BEN TURNER IS A DEAD MAN

BY

RYAN BRACHA

PUBLISHED BY

Abrachadabra
Books

IN ASSOCIATION WITH

PADDY'S DADDY PUBLISHING

FOR REBECCA AND
DELILAH. MY GIRLS.

PROLOGUE

THE RAIN smashed repeatedly against his back, like a barrage of miniature fists. Each one an angry missile from the sky with an apparent grudge against him and only him. The wind didn't help matters. An ice cold wall of Mother Nature's hatred for all things man. It lashed at him relentlessly. Punishing him for his crimes. He didn't stop though. Darkness was his cloak. He needed these hours of invisibility. He couldn't ever trust the light to hold him safe. Not yet. Not until he got there. His enemies were everywhere. They knew his face. They knew his name. They knew his crime. He was less than a mile from the wall. He pulled the bag around from his back, squeezed the thing. Felt for the corners of his secrets. They were still there. Wrapped in several layers of polythene, cotton, polyester, canvas. He pushed relief through his lips on the crest of a sigh and swung the bag back onto his shoulder, and pressed on. If it were only the wind that had it in for him he might have been grateful for the assistance along the road. But the rain. It continued to strike him ferociously. Relentlessly. Reminded him just how unwanted he was in this country. A light appeared in the distance. Two lights. A car. With a pained gasp he made to sidestep from the road but his left ankle conspired with the elements and gave way beneath him, his leg rolling over on it and tossing his dripping wet body into a relatively dry ditch, given the weather. The desperate man cried out in pain as the corner of his secrets jutted into his back but he couldn't move. The rumble of the vehicle drew nearer. The agony of his ankle throbbed a heavy beat against the rapid percussion of the rain smashing against his face. Still the vehicle chugged ever closer to him. He doubted that they'd see him down there. Although the ditch was shallow the night gave him his cover almost as well as the long reed-like grass which ran the edge of it. But he still dare not move. The crunch of the wheels against the uneven road surface grew louder. Louder still. The desperate man closed his eyes, as if shutting the world out from himself might offer a favour returned. The fat rain thumped his eyelids so hard that each impact created a minor but harsh sting in his eyes. Then as steadily as the sound increased it began to decrease. The car, van, whatever, had passed. The rain slowed. The desperate man lay still in his cover. The wind continued to whistle in the barren moorland, but that rain. It had thinned. Not to a complete stop but it improved life for him to an infinite degree. He waited until the vehicle had gone from the area completely, and sat up. He pulled his secrets once again to his hands. Pressed against the corner which had until then been attempting to burrow into his kidney. It remained intact. Thanking the almighty whoever, the desperate man dragged himself up the small bank of the dry ditch. Attempted to place pressure on his sprained ankle. Only a small amount of pain. It felt okay. Not great, but okay, and for a man in his position, okay would have to do. He hoped, prayed that he could walk it off. A cursory sweep of the area showed him to be alone once again. Less than a mile. It's all that stood between he, and something else altogether. He wasn't exactly sure what, but it had to be a better prospect than what faced him here. He stepped tentatively along the road, pressing as little pressure on his injured ankle

Ryan Bracha

as possible, before the silhouette of his destiny appeared in the night before him. The wall. The desperate man whimpered desperately, pulling himself away from the road and into the soaking grassland. Beneath him the sodden grass squelched, and sucked at the soles of his boots, hungrily attempting to take the things right from his feet. Each limp toward the wall was a limp toward his destiny. Toward his freedom. He knew that the wall wasn't particularly expert-built, given that it was rushed together by convicts with little or no building experience, so there were parts of it which would be easier to traverse than others. He had done his homework, and he knew what he wanted. The road that he had travelled up on disappeared further and further behind him, along with his past, and he reached the wall, beyond which lay his future. The desperate man placed his forehead against the cold wet brickwork of the wall, muttering laboured words of thanks, and appreciation. He placed two hands flat against it, and raised his eyes to the sky. The rain had dissipated further, and had become a misty fog of moisture. No real rain as such, but the air around him was sodden. The wind, too, had slowed. The wall offered enough of a barrier from the elements that he was afforded space in his skull for thought. His eyes skirted the length of the wall to his right, until they reached the floodlit security building. He couldn't go that way. Too close. To the left the wall stretched deep into the night and the countryside. It was his only option. He trudged heavily along the length of the wall. Constantly scanning for foot-holes, or jagged metalwork, anything which might allow him to climb the thing. Eventually he found what he was looking for. It was a spot notorious for border-jumpers. In the middle of the day he'd never have a chance to making of, there would be far too much security patrolling the area. But tonight, in this weather, in this darkness and at this time, conditions were perfect. The night time border security staff were well known by his former employer for their ineptitude, but they were simply for show. Anybody that skipped the border was dealt with by a stronger and harsher force deeper into the country. The crews. The desperate man breathed deeply. With one hand he grabbed a hole of a rusted iron rod jutting from the brickwork. Pulled himself up. Placed a foot on another rod. Slowly but surely clambered up the face of the wall, holding onto his secrets as tightly as possible. He couldn't lose them. Not now. Not after he'd got so far. He hoisted his body up on to the top of the wall, and with relief his exhaled hard into the sky. He laid flat on the narrow roof of the wall and for the first time in days he laughed. He closed his eyes and he laughed through relief, and through incredulity. He'd made it. He was at the border, and he was now out of the former employer's jurisdiction. He-

"Whit the fuck dae we have here?" said a voice from above him. He winced at the coarse vulgarity. It was not an English accent. The desperate man slowly and fearfully opened his eyes. Two faces looked down at him. In the dark they weren't young faces. Maybe his own age, but he conceded that it really was dark. He didn't move.

"Sumbdy tryin' tae get intae oor land eh?" the other man said.

"Could be," the first man said, before turning his attention downwards, "so who the fuck might you be, and whit the fuck are ye daen' tryin' tae get intae oor country, big man?"

The desperate man sighed, and without wishing to cause too much alarm spoke softly.

Ryan Bracha

"I'm looking for somebody," he said, "he's in your country."

The second of the men leant further in, and grinned malevolently.

"An' whit makes ye think that we'll let ye get intae oor fuckin' country, tae look fir ye pal, eh?"

The desperate man winced once again, but without a second thought lifted his boot up, and hard, to connect with the crotch of his questioner. The man yelped in agony, bowed over as far as it needed for the desperate man to take a hold of his collar, and cast him down from the wall onto the soft ground below. With one down he scrambled to his feet and balanced precariously along the top of the wall, and faced his remaining assailant.

"Please, I don't wish you any harm, but two on one was rather unfair odds."

The first man stood in stunned silence, his lip in the dark appearing to quiver in the first stages of what is known as crying.

"Whit ye dae that for, eh?" he said, looking confused, and angry.

"I told you, unfair odds. Now listen to me. I've travelled a long time to get here, and I won't let you stop me, but I'm prepared to let you help. I'm looking for a man. He came to your country a few days ago, and I need to see him. He goes by the name of Carter. Paul Carter."

CHAPTER ONE

Somewhere in Yorkshire.

Slap.
The chubby law man's face ripples as the effects of my forceful strike take their hold. My hands grip his cheeks to halt the mesmerising wave of flesh, and I pull his jowls close. I smile at him as I speak.
"Awright there pal?" I say, with no hint of actual concern in my mocking tones, "feart eh?"
"Sorry?"
"Ah asked if ye were feart, feart ay a girl?"
"I don't know what you're saying."
Slap. Whimper. Silence. I look to my back up of six men, who are holding two other of the chubby law man's colleagues firm between them, roll my eyes, and return my gaze to the portly crew member. I sigh.
"Ah said, are ye jackin' *scared* ay a girl the now? Are ye doin' a wee bit ay sherbet in ye pants? Cause ah'm tellin' ye now, ye jackin' should be. Yer no makin' it oot ay this here situation alive. There's gonnae be some changes around here, and there needs tae be somebody we can make a wee example of. Rab Lodge's gonnae come a cropper soon, you mark ma words. Paul Carter's gonnae make sure ay that. So am gonnae ask ye one more time, are ye feart, *Simon?*"
Between the firm grip of my fingers he attempts a nod. Against his will tears begin to ball up in his deep, red eyes. He tries to speak.
"Pluh-"
Nothing. I've got him held too tightly.
"Eh?" I say, loosening my grip on his face.
"Please, don't-"

"Naw, dinnae you start greetin', or beggin', cause it's gonnae dae ye nae good, yer a dead man Simon, ah'm just a wee bit fond ay the dramatic, if ah were you ah'd hold ma head up high an' take what's comin' tae me, go oot with a wee bit ay self-respect."

No use. Simon's weeping, the tears snaking down his cheek, and over the manicured hot pink nails which grip deeper into his skin. Upon the cooling touch of the salty droplets I shift and lower my grip. I let my hand fall a few inches, and reach back in to hold onto Simon's neck, before squeezing onto his oesophagus, digging my nails in behind the ribbed tube. Simon gargles. Tries to fight against the arms which hold him steady. Tries to kick out but to no avail. The intense pain of his throat being crushed beneath my firm hold sends his nervous system into meltdown. He thrashes but not for long, before he's lowered to the ground by his captors. From the ground, and in his final seconds, his glassy eyes register me drop a heavy boot onto his neck and crush any remaining life from his body. Had he any life left he might well have also witness me punch his colleague to the floor, and smash his skull to almost nothing against the pavement. I stop only to breathe, and laugh hard at the third remaining crew member. A dark stain of urine pitching a contrast against the light brownish khaki pants. I stand from my lethal endeavour, still giggling through heavy breaths, and draw a flinch from my captive as I push my face hard into his. My nose touching his, my eyes staring deep into his soul. Blood drips violently from my shaking hands.

"You're a lucky piece of sherbet ma boy, you're the jackin' *messenger,* you run on back to Mr James Finnegan, and you tell him we're not finished, not by a *long* chalk. You tell him that Paul Carter's army are comin', and you tell him that if Mr Robert Lodge thinks his wee nightmare is over now Carter's in Scotland, he can jackin' think again. This wee perty's just gettin' started."

I nod to Monty and Jacques, who loosen their hold on the law man, allowing him to wriggle free, and beat a hasty retreat from us all; his desperate sobs echo high into the cold night, drowned out eventually by my laughter. When he's finally gone from our lives I quieten, turning to the others.

"Well, that was fun," I say, with all hint of Scottish disappearing from my accent, "seriously; it's been ages since I had that much fun."

Jacques laughs uneasily, but says nothing.

"Do you think they'll buy it Nat?" asks Monty, a weasel faced wiry man whose twisted moustache not so much hints at upper class as it does climb aboard an open top bus and declare it through a loud speaker. I shrug, an easy smile on my face.

"Probably, who knows? My accent was bloody good though wasn't it?" I say, wiping the blood from my victim's skull back onto his insignia clad jacket, "anyway, what's the worst that can happen if they don't? We just have to keep going until they pay attention."

A moment of post-coital reflection.

I watch the smoke curl and swirl lazily away from the end of my cigarette, before it is suddenly ripped from its languid efforts by the force of the open window of the car. I love these moments of post-coital reflection that I get after a kill. My heart rate dropping back to normal, the last of the adrenaline seeping through my pores. I ponder Simon's face, his chubby twitching features that grew ever more erratic when he realised that the life he was living was about to get cut quite dramatically short. Marvellous stuff, simply marvellous.

"Penny for them, Nat?" asks Monty as his eyes dart to me from the road briefly. I realise that I've been smiling.

"Just doing some remembering is all Monty, you know how it is."

"You've some blood on your cheek," he says, passing his monogrammed handkerchief my way.

"Thanks," I say, rubbing at my cheek, before presenting it to my friend, "did I get it?"

He glances my way again and nods, so I relax once more into my seat, and pull my boot up to the dashboard.

"So what's the plan now?" he asks.

"I don't know, I could do with something to eat," I shrug, to the rattling of a packet in the back. A bag of salt and vinegar crisps come flying over my shoulder and bounce into the foot well.

"Best I can do, Nat," says Julian, who's a simply marvellous boy. I turn to smile my appreciation, and reach to grab-

SMASH

Suddenly my world rotates through several revolutions. A cacophonous noise rattles into my consciousness, and a shower of glass rains down on me from all angles. Our car spins once, and I feel a boot to the jaw from the lifeless flopping body of Julian. It spins twice and our heads crack together. At the third spin, through the blood that pours into my eyes I see his mangled body hanging, crushed and broken out of the back passenger side window. The car finally comes to a halt after the fourth spin, and on its head. A haze of semi-consciousness floats into my world, as I hang from my seat, my only protection against gravity is my seat belt. Monty is unconscious and dangling in much the same position as me. I don't know what's happened. There's a tap tap tapping in the back, of Julian's blood onto the ceiling of the car, and a hissing of some part of the engine dying. Suddenly there are voices. Loud, panicked voices. I can vaguely recognise one as Barnaby, and another of Gerard. They're shouting at somebody, or something. My hands snake up to my seat belt slowly, searching for the lock. I don't know why I press it but I do, and my body falls heavily onto the ceiling, and I drag myself laboriously through the broken window. From my viewpoint on the floor, I see them. I see them strike Barnaby first. He goes to the ground and they descend upon him like jackals. Gerard makes an attempt to save our friend but they take him too. Francis and Kenneth try to run. Francis makes it as far as the other car before he is stopped in his tracks by a Taser to the back. He falls, twitching and spazzing out on the floor. Kenneth doesn't make it that far before another of them takes him down in the same way. A tall man in a leather jacket strides over to them, and pulls out a knife. I want to scream out but I can't. A silent call for him to show them mercy goes unsaid, and unheard. He draws the knife across Kenneth's throat, and then he strides to Francis and treats him to more of the same. Then he sees me, and he smiles. I try to drag myself away but I can't. My arms don't want to help me, my legs are on strike. Instead I watch as the tall man in the leather jacket stomps purposefully toward me. Behind him his own crew stand nonchalantly, trusting him to do it all himself. He squats beside me, and I close my eyes to await my fate. A moment passes, and then another. Nothing. I hear him moving around me, but he doesn't touch me. A familiar noise. The crisp packet. As he rips it open I open my eyes. His fingers dig hungrily into the pack, and he sits beside me, cross-legged. His eyes sparkle with mischief beneath his closely cropped hair and sweating forehead, as he jams the crisps into his mouth.

"Salt and vinegar, I *love* salt and vinegar," he says between crunching bites, and sucking the flavour from his fingers, "I'm Ben, by the way," he says as he grabs my hand and shakes it rigorously, "you've been a naughty bitch, Miss Sweeney."

A naughty bitch.

He's not wrong. I *have* been naughty. Very naughty. But I wasn't always. I used to be quite the opposite, until the bomb.

In my old life I was a lawyer, a quite well respected and successful family lawyer. I was at one point the most sought after family lawyer in London. Celebrities and sports stars alike would clamour after my services in dividing parents and children. When the regime changed I opted to remain in the UK to keep hold of the family land, and stand as one of the best lawyers in the country. What I didn't foresee unfortunately, was the change in law enforcement. Courts and law were dismantled. The right of judge and jury belonged to the people. Myself, Monty, Gerard and the rest were put to work in steel works and mines. My family land was ripped from my grasp by *pretend-Britons* who thought my house was better than theirs. My cash was taken from me by the government, and I was left with nothing but the pittance in Network credits I would earn from my job. Over the years we built up a heavy steam of disgruntlement with our newly allotted role in society, and when a man called Paul Carter decided to throw the proverbial cat into the pigeons six months ago and kick-start an uprising, we took our chance to disappear from the radar. What we didn't expect was that shortly after that, our Prime Minister Robert Lodge took our country to war with Scotland, or No-Man's Land, depending on who you're talking to, and once again the country united against a common cause.

What Paul did.

I suppose I should probably explain a few things about six months ago. You know? In case you're joining the party a little late. I won't hold it against you at all, just bear in mind that in my old life you'd be paying through the nose for this time I'm giving to you. For free.

In New Britain, we live our lives on The Network, which is an all-encompassing, life-enhancing social media platform. On The Network we can order our food shopping, play electronic games, gamble, watch audio-visual treats such as the soapbox comedians like Johnny Stiff and Biscuit Billy, or the immensely popular talent scouting channel devised and run by the flamboyant Baz le Shaz. We can comment on forums, or make our own private diaries. Arguably most popular of all, and what most people get up for in the morning, is judging. This is what happened to our precious law and order. Our justice system. My former life. There are organisations that have been contracted by the government to catch and parade criminals, these organisations are called *crews.* I know, very crass. The crews will parade criminals for twenty four hours on The Crime Network, and we the public are given twenty four hours to choose whether they are guilty or not guilty, and punishment is only a click away. It's not gone amiss by your sweet narrator that ninety per cent of these criminals will be judged guilty, and probably ninety per cent of those are innocent of what we used to call crimes, in the old days.

What Robert Lodge did was offer an exchange. In exchange for this power, he requested that we lived by what he called The Guidelines. These rules were basically a convoluted series of morals that he imposed upon us, essentially forcing us to live by his own fudged up standards. You see I say fudged instead of a baser alternative? That's because no swearing is one of The Guidelines. It makes no difference, we just switch the original with a quickly thought up alternative. As long as the tone is right, you can switch it with any word. I'm going to put my dunking foot right up your marmalade you jacking gherkin. See?

So what Paul Carter did was he killed somebody. Some troll that affected his reputation. He held his hands up and admitted he did it and why, but what got up people's noses the most was that he then went on to kill a member of a Government Authorised Crew whilst making his escape. I know, I was horrified about it myself at the time myself, I mean, you just can't do that. Swearing is one thing, but murder was another thing all together. We all voiced our hatred for Paul Carter on The Network, said what we'd do to him if we got our hands on him, but then he did something quite remarkable. He, and a small group of supporters, some say army but I'm not sure they were even classed as a gang there were so few of them; anyway, they took their fight to the government. They broke into the headquarters of the now defunct Network Cutting Crew, and exposed their leader, a man named Wilson Becker, as a violent thug who carried illegal firearms. Now, Robert Lodge is a man of principles if nothing else. He had Becker judged and executed for his flagrant abuse of power, but Carter and his team escaped. Some people say he went to Scotland, others say he crafted a boat from raw materials he found on his crusade and either made it to Ireland or he drowned trying. Whatever happened to him, his name lives on. His legacy, his legend. I'm going to make sure of that.

Against the backdrop of the ridiculous and pointless war we've spent our time fighting from the inside. We call in crimes, and when the Government Authorised Network Crews show up, well that's when we strike. We cannot afford for Robert Lodge to claim a stronghold on our country again. If he does then we're jacked. We made it our life's work to strike fear into the government, to try to keep the momentum of Paul Carter's legacy going. So far we have killed upwards of twenty five crew members across the country. I say we, it was all me. You have no idea how satisfying it is. You might call me a monster for my crimes, but I'm no monster. I'm simply a woman who made a poor decision in the interests of money, and now I'm taking my pound of flesh back from every bandstand who wronged me, and I won't stop until I get all the way to the top, and rip Robert Lodge's head from his snivelling dunking shoulders. Oh, who am I kidding? I am a monster, I'm a dunking animal.

Back in the present.

"How do you know my name?" I ask of the mysterious Ben who remains seated by my side, still crunching down on the crisps. He smiles gormlessly.
"You're Nat Sweeney, you're pretty fuckin' recognisable," he says, "you know how much jizz I

wasted over pictures of you in your tight little suits back in my old life?"

I recoil for a number of reasons here. For one, the use of profanity. For two, that he recognises me. For three, the disgusting vision he has just given me, the misogynistic rucksack.

"I'm only kidding," he chuckles, "I've only done it once, when they showed me your picture."

I grimace.

"Oh, come on, you've got eyes, right? You know how fit you are."

"Why don't you just kill me and then go and dunk yourself?"

"Why don't I kill you, and then dunk *you?* Long as you're still warm, right? I can do both our voices, pretend you're loving it. *Oh, Ben, you're so big, that's one gigantic cock you have, I bet I could get it in my tight dead arsehole,*" he says the last part in some ridiculous mocking version of my own well-spoken accent. I'm not going to indulge the cupcake so I close my eyes and I sigh, but this only makes him chuckle. He's *so* infuriating. I change the subject.

"Why did you kill them?" I ask.

"Kill who?"

"My men," I say, "they were my friends."

"I didn't kill your friends," he laughs, "except that one," he says, pointing at the limp and broken corpse of Julian, "but that was an accident. He should have been wearing his fuckin' seatbelt."

I shake my head, and eyeball him with hatred.

"No, I saw you, you killed them, all of them," I growl, but the bemused look on his face continues to irritate me, I would love to stomp on his throat right now.

"Who?" he asks, "them?" He moves from my line of sight by shuffling on his backside along the floor, and they're all there, lined up and alive by the side of his people carrier. But I saw them. I saw what he did to them. I feel relief wash over me but at the same time I really don't know what's happening. Did I just imagine that?

"But," is all I can say, before I'm overcome by a gentle nausea and I drift out of consciousness.

SIX MONTHS AGO

"Seriously, ah dinnae ken who yer talkin' aboot pal, aw ah do is walk up and down these waws, make sure nane ay you skanky English shitebags sneak yer way in. You guard yer roads tae make sure we dinnae escape. I tell you what, we dinnae well fuckin' want tae escape!"

The desperate man sighed in frustration. Pinched his nose. Focused on the Scotsman again.

"Okay, so you're quite the primitive. Well the boy Carter has been big news, and the word is that he's here. You can't tell me where he is but I'm damned sure there's somebody that can. Take me to Davie Craig."

The Scotsman visibly recoiled in shock briefly before breaking into hysterics.

"Ye reckon ye can just walk up tae Davie Craig's big hoose in E'nburgh an' say how d'ye dae? Yer oot ay yer nut pal."

Edinburgh.

"I'll worry about that when we get there, just take me to Edinburgh."

The desperate man struggled to maintain composure as he watched the Scotsman's features firm up. He shook his head.

"Ah'm afraid ah cannae help."

"A loyal man, eh? I was loyal once. It gets you nowhere."

The desperate man punched the Scotsman hard in the face, stunning him enough to throw the man down to his unconscious friend on the New British side of the wall. Without wasting a second thought, he quickly climbed down onto the Scottish side and began his next gruelling task of traversing the path to

Edinburgh. Hoping to God that the two men he'd just assaulted had left a vehicle of some sort, *with* keys, up the road he headed in the direction of the A1 motorway. Holding on to his secrets tighter than ever now he was on the most dangerous and untested soil he'd set foot on for over five years. The vehicle was indeed up the road, as hoped, but unfortunately the owners had the foresight to take their keys with them, costing the desperate man five minutes delay in starting the thing. Another hope he had, was that the men he'd just assaulted didn't have radios, and hadn't just warned the entire country that Harry Garner, former second-in-command of the country of New Britain, had just physically attacked two of their men and was headed for their leader.

In all honesty, Garner hoped that it didn't actually need to reach the ears of Davie Craig. He would much rather it remained off his radar and between him and Carter. His necessary actions recently had jeopardised that hope, but the best he could do was go on as planned, and if he and Craig locked horns then he would have to deal with that at the time, there was no point fearing the worst.

Little over two hours later he was entering Edinburgh, scarcely able to comprehend what he was seeing. The city appeared to be thriving. People were walking amongst one another, even at this early hour. People clambered lazily from their vehicles to get into offices. A refuse truck bleeped urgently to warn pedestrians of its reversing status as bin men lofted black bags into its hungry back. Like everywhere else in the world. Everywhere except New Britain. Here, nobody walked with a Network device in their hands. Harry Garner pulled the car into a side street, and launched himself from the seat as he vomited what little food there was in his stomach up onto the cold

Scottish ground. Edinburgh was like London used to be, years ago, when he was a young teenager. Before he ever met Robert Lodge. The early seventies.

Garner edged back into the car, gasping the taste of vomit away from his mouth, and placed a hand upon the bag that contained his secrets with a sigh. With a recently instilled sense of premature defeat, Harry Garner sparked the ignition of the car, and began his arduous task of finding the only man who could help him. Even if he did find him, however, there was no guarantee that he *would*.

CHAPTER TWO

Somewhere more familiar.

My foot crunches onto the pebbles and broken glass of the car park that they've brought us to. The car park itself belongs to what appears to be a disused police station. If it's an ironic gesture I couldn't tell. Jacques holds me up as I laboriously limp toward the building, up ahead Kenneth is offering the same service to Monty. None of Ben's own crew has uttered a word to any of us at all, seemingly allowing Ben to be the entire group's mouthpiece. I imagine that he likes it that way, since he seems to want to marry his own voice. He struts around like he's the coolest man alive, and I'll be honest with you, he's not. He's a sweaty, quite probably prematurely balding weasel of a man, who wears a leather jacket which is too big. It's like he stole it from the corpse of a man who was two sizes broader than him, and quite probably carried the look a lot better than he does. The whole procession of us being herded toward the building goes on in silence but for pained grunts from me and Monty, the crunching of boots against messy concrete, and Ben muttering things to one of his men, seemingly in amusement. We get to around twenty metres from the building and Ben halts us.
"Now, I know you're all wondering what the fuck is going on, and some of you are probably scared for your lives," he looks pointedly at me when he says that last part, "but don't worry your pretty little heads," he winks at me, I want five minutes along with the pringle, show him what real scared for your life looks like, "if you play ball you'll be out of here

soon enough. I just can't have you fuckin' my hard work up, like the fuckin' amateurs that you are."

Before I get a chance to be infuriated by the last sentence, my eyes are caught by some bright green graffiti declaring that we should *Keep Britian Brittish,* and a shiver toys with my spine. If this is a *Pretend British* stronghold then we're probably all in trouble. Ben catches me looking at it.

"A friend of mine did that," he says, a proud look on his face, "*on purpose.*"

"Big whoop," I say, as unimpressed as I am, I force twenty levels more of unimpressed into my tone, "did you friend buy you the jacket too?"

What the pretenders did next.

In the wake of Paul Carter's acts of treason, one group of people have been more prone than anybody else to acting up. The Pretend British population. They've not just taken his ideology and run with it, they've made it their life's work. When Robert Lodge came to power and offered them all the in-or-out ultimatum, they played ball as much as it suited them. Yes, there were the territorial hazards of a night time foray out into the open, but they stuck to the guidelines. They had to, because as much as a unified Britain was the dream, if you were a *Pretender* then you stood no chance if you were up for judgement. I looked it up once, and literally one hundred per cent of Pretenders was judged guilty on The Crime Network. One hundred per cent. Not ninety nine point nine. One hundred. That tells you as much as you need to know about the way our country is, was, whatever. So when law enforcement was exposed as being quite vulnerable, not to mention more than just a little corrupted, the Pretend British population milked it for all it was worth. I'm sure you're sensing a little hypocrisy from me, talking about them doing it when I'm doing the same thing, but you'd be wrong. I'm not judging them, I'm merely stating facts.

The war with Scotland-
I probably ought to tell you about the war with Scotland oughtn't I? There's no point telling you about something if you don't have the full story.

The war.

Six months ago Robert Lodge declared war on No-Man's Land. He said it was because groups of people from north of the border were killing crew members. He said that it was a threat to national security. He said that the cannibals were dripping down from beyond the wall, and that we needed to stand up against them. Thousands of men and women emerged from behind their tablet computers to stand up and be counted. Government Authorised Crews would donate several teams of men to pour forth and fight the monsters from Scotland. Newcastle suddenly became the place to be, Lancaster to a lesser degree. Those cities teemed with fresh faced young men and women who rubbed shoulders with the former fighters from when our country had an actual army, an actual navy, and an actual air force; they were all keen to support their country's endeavours against the uncouth monsters beyond the wall. Rupert Green, the man behind the man that was Robert Lodge, led the charge in that he stood at the back and directed these youngsters to their deaths. Lodge had removed lethal firearms from our country long before the war had started; it was something to do with the law men, something about removing the potential for rogue elements. I think Wilson Becker proved that theory dead right. Anyway, the armies charged the wall, only to be met by crude barbarians who stopped at nothing to ensure New British blood was spilled. This continued for three months, before Robert Lodge not so much admitted defeat, more gave the impression that he was bored with it all, and the defeat of the Scots could wait. I'm not exaggerating when I say the number of New British deaths reached four figures in such a short space of time.

One thing that concerned me throughout the whole three months of carnage and bloodshed was the total lack of outside interference. Back when we were a paid up and active member of the global council, a Middle Eastern despot couldn't so much as step on the toes of somebody in the supermarket before our Prime Minister, or the President of America came wading in with threats of war. Showing that we were the big boys coming to the defence of the weak child with the calliper and the respiratory disease. So, when our own despot charges his own people to their deaths against a merciless and barbaric race such as the Scots, where was the intervention then? Call me a cynic, but I wouldn't be surprised if Robert Lodge was still very much in touch with the rest of the world, despite what he demanded of us.

You know who he is, don't you?

The door clicks shut, leaving me and Monty on one side of it, in a small dark cell, and one of our silent captors on the other, slipping the key into the lock and shutting us in for the foreseeable future. There's a tiny inch-thick window set into the top of the wall at the far end of the cell which allows a surprising amount of light into our space. Years of attempts by whoever to smash the thing with rocks has left most of it chipped and scratched, with a hole in the centre of it. The breeze whistles against this small maw, making the room feel colder than it actually is. Neither Monty, nor I say anything for a short while, as at least for my part I'm not really sure what there is to say. I play the events of the last few hours out quickly in my head, breaking it down to bullet points for brevity's sake, an old tactic that I employed in my old life as a lawyer, and something which I find hard to shake.

- We attack the crew members, leaving them in no doubt that Paul Carter is coming for them.
- We're ambushed by a mysterious and quite garrulous rucksack by the name of Ben with a band of not quite so chatty men, who seems to know exactly who I am, and has been *given* a photo of me. Which means we were targeted.
- We're fetched to some abandoned police station in Sheffield where Ben claims to know people who have daubed graffiti onto it, where we are then placed in cells and find ourselves at right now.

I'm not sure I'm getting anything here. We were targeted, but I can't for the life of me think by whom. I need some time with Ben alone I think, see if I can't beat the information from him.

"You know who he is, don't you?" asks Monty, watching me in amusement.

"Who *who* is?" I say.

"Our ambusher, Mr Ben Turner."

I shake my head again. The name sounds familiar, but not so much that it leaps out.

"No, do you?"

"Oh my, yes. He's one fifth of the reason we're doing what we are."

Monty does this, offers somewhat cryptic responses when a solid chunk of information at once would suffice.

"Monty, just tell me," I say, I'd like to add that I don't have time for it, but who am I kidding? We could be here for weeks yet.

"Ben Turner, he's Paul Carter's right hand man, I can't believe you don't recognise him."

Oh Christ. I feel the blood drain from my face like the water in a freshly opened canal lock. What the hell would Ben Turner want with us? And perhaps more importantly, how long before Paul Carter shows up? I feel my throat constrict and I battle my gag reflex. I do believe we've just made it to the big leagues.

Mr Turner.

Ben Turner used to be a mischief maker with an extraordinary passion for upsetting Wilson Becker. He would flagrantly harass the Network Cutting Crew, hurling profanity without fear, and he would break every minor law just to get under the skin of their now-dead leader. He'd never go so far as to commit major acts of violence, he just liked to make points about the pettiness of some of The Guidelines. He would be placed up for judgement, and spend his twenty four hours acting the goat, bringing attention to the ridiculous nature of his being there at all. Seven times he was placed up for judgement, eight if you include his dramatic escape effort, and the public loved him for it. Each time they spent more time watching his performances, rather than taking the time to judge him. I think he reminded them of the old days, when people loved an eccentric rebel. Somebody who just seemed to get away with it, every time.

Nobody knows how or why he got involved with Paul Carter, but he did, and from then he became a different beast all together. He'd been given the keys to the sweety factory, and he took to it like a duck to water. I heard that he'd beaten two crew members to death when he was *handcuffed.* I heard that he'd spent the next few hours spitting into the mouths of crew members that he'd knocked unconscious, sharing his Hepatitis with as many of them as he could. That's what the official line on it is, anyway, and I find it hard not to believe it.

So he disappeared when Carter and the rest did, and again it was presumed that they'd either fled the country through the wall to Scotland, by boat to Ireland, or been killed trying either. Whichever of the escape stories is likeliest, it doesn't matter, he's back now, and he's got us held hostage. Some small part of me is shipping myself, but there's a whole solid majority chunk of me which is excited as Hell to meet the man.

So now I know.

"Oh, Monty, this is big," I say, a huge smile across my face as I pace the small area of floor that we're afforded in the cell. Monty has seated himself on the edge of a drop-down bed which was previously strapped to the wall. His fingers nervously toy with the ends of his moustache.
"I agree, Nat, but come on. This man killed indiscriminately," he says.

"And we didn't?" I counter.

"We?" he asks, a pointed look in his eyes.

"Okay, *I* didn't? I bet I've done more to put the ships up the law than he ever did. The only difference is that we were smarter. We were quieter. He just *has* to make a big song and dance about it. This," I say, sweeping my hand around the room, and beyond to illustrate my point, "is what he's all about. He had to take us hostage, make some stupid point about knowing who I was, to *prove* that he was smarter. He's not smarter, he's just a showman. They're not going to kill any of us."

"What makes you so sure?"

"Because he needs us, that's why, he knows what we're capable of. I'm not just talking about me killing people. He needs the whole package, all of us. I bet you that the reason half of his men aren't talking to us is because they're so dumb that he's made sure they say nothing for fear of saying something stupid."

Monty shakes his head doubtfully.

"I wouldn't be so sure," he says, his beady eyes darting around like they do. Peeking out from beneath the greying skin of his face.

"Well, what do you think?" I ask, offering him his chance to make whatever it is that's rattling around his mind known.

"I don't know, I just don't see it being as easy as that," he mutters.

"Oh, come on, Monty! Where's my friend gone? Where's the Monty I knew who could rip a confession from the innocent without even breaking a sweat? Where's Montgomery McFarlane?" I say playfully and affectionately. He's known to wobble on occasion, but I think that's just an age thing. He's obviously not the spring chicken he once was, but I know for a fact that

the man's mind is still one hundred per cent lethal.
He shakes his head dolefully.
"I'm not sure it's one of those times, I'm afraid, Nat."

Elsewhere.

He'd been running for well over two hours. The
blisters on his heels and toes rubbed agonisingly
against the inside of his tight boots. The sharp nail on
the second toe of his right foot, that he'd been
threatening to cut for weeks, sliced deep into the soft
flesh of his big toe. He wanted to stop but he daren't.
They could be following him. Ready to pounce when
he paused. His heart laid heavy breeze block punches
into the inner of his rib cage. His armpits burned sore
from the rubbing of his polyester uniform. His mouth
was dry as sandpaper since the moisture in his body
had priorities elsewhere, in his tear ducts and sweat
glands. Still he didn't stop though. He ran, and he ran.
A van carrying members of the Tough Justice
Network Crew slowed and chugged alongside him as
he ran. He afforded a glance to the passenger
windows, to see sneering and amused faces from
crew members who watched him. What must they
have seen? A weeping, snot-faced Finnegan Law
Enforcement crew member running alone. Surely
they should stop? No. They wouldn't. They were
Tough Justice. The competition. Instead one of them
wound his window down, hollered that he was a total
pansy, and told him to man up. Then they sped away,
the laughter of four crew members echoing into the
night. After tonight he was out. There was nothing
they could put on him to convince him to stay. They
could put him up for judgement; they could stick him
with an UnBritish Behaviour charge. They could do as
they pleased, but watching two of his closest friends

cut down in the line of duty by some No-Man's Land backpacks closed off any loyalty he had to the job. He would pass on her message, and he would walk out of there, nothing more said. Still he ran, and cried, and sweated, and bled, and ran some more.

Enter Mr Robert Lodge.

"Green, what is it?"
"Sir, we have received a call from the office of James Finnegan."
"And?"
"He has lost two men today to a roaming gang of vigilantes."
"Oh dear."
"Quite."
"And what can I do about it?"
"I'm not sure, sir. The gang did allow one of the crew members to escape though. He said a woman let him go."
"*A woman?* But why would they do that?"
"To send a message, sir."
"A message?"
"Yes, sir."
"To whom?"
"..."
"Green?"
"To you, sir."
"To me?"
"Yes, sir."
"And what did this message pertain to?"
"Ehm, I shall quote the crew member verbatim, sir. *Tell them that Paul Carter's army is coming.*"
"Carter?"
"Yes, sir."

Ben Turner is a Dead Man

"To be quite honest, Green, Carter's *army* last time wasn't much more than a gang, and ultimately all they did was expose a corrupt crew leader and then disappear, I wouldn't place too much stock in the threat of a girl, Green. Just have an extra man placed on the gates."

"Sir?"

"What?"

"It's just that the vigilantes had quite distinctive accents, sir."

"Scouse?"

"No, sir. No-Man's Land."

"Again? Well, I'm not going to have *a woman* send me running scared, not at all, have an extra two men put on the gates, and don't bother me with this again."

"As you wish, sir."

SIX MONTHS AGO

Garner entered the sandwich shop, nervously checking for other patrons before approaching the slender man behind the counter. The man offered a friendly smile, which melted into suspicion as Garner opened his mouth.

"Yes, ehm, a neeps and tatty sandwich, please." He had no clue what he was ordering, only that these people made a tradition of eating it, so it seemed a good place to start. To try to blend in with the natives. It appeared to have been a grand error when the man's face twisted into disdain, then dropped heavily into disgust territory.

"Eh? Fuckin' neeps an' tatty oan a fuckin' butty? Are ye takin' the fuckin' pish?"

"Ehm, haggis then, please? And would you mind awfully not using such vulgar language?"

"Naw, man. Yer takin' the fuckin' pish oot ay ma fuckin' country. An' this is ma fuckin' butty shop, so ah c'n use whichever fuckin' language ah want. Ye c'n either leave through the front fuckin' door or ah c'n chuck ye oot ay that fuckin' windae. The choice is yours, son."

Garner winced. Thus far he'd made a grand mess of the whole thing. All he'd wanted to do was get some information about Carter's whereabouts without having to resort to violence. So far he'd assaulted two men, and was skirting very close to having to do it again. He set his secrets down upon the floor by his feet, in an attempt to show the man that he intended to go nowhere.

"Look, I don't mean any trouble. Really I don't. I'm looking for somebody here in Edinburgh."

"Ah dinnae give two fucks sunshine," said the proprietor, reaching down behind the counter to retrieve a grease smeared knife, and holding it in the direction of the unfortunate Englishman, he rounded the counter and spoke, "ye c'n be lookin' fir the meanin' ay life itself, but ah'm gi'in ye nowt. So ah'm askin' ye again. Windae or door?"

Garner lowered his head and sighed. He'd played nice. He'd been civil and calm. He hoped the proprietor would stay where he was but he didn't. He continued in a stride which said the knife would be embedded in Garner's gut long before he made the decision with which he'd be tasked. As the man raised a hand to lay it down on Garner's shoulder he was surprised when his potential victim twisted on his heels deftly before reaching up to take a hold of the fingers and crunching them together as if they were as significant as a crisp packet. The proprietor wailed in anguish and dropped his knife, before dropping to the floor himself, nursing his broken digits through snotty tears.

"Whit the fuck ye dae that for?" he whined as Garner lowered himself to pick up the knife, and then a handful of the sandwich man's hair, dragging him upright. The man continued to focus on his fingers and sniffed back the rapidly developing snot in his nose.

"Broke ma fingers, man, ah wisnae gonnae shank ye or nowt, ah wis just messin' aboot. Ma fuckin' fingers."

"Please, stop swearing, it's very unbecoming," said Garner, edging the backwards, until he eventually met a chair by a table covered in blue and white chequered cloth and a variety of condiments. The man continued wept gently in the chair, uttering a repetition of his finger woes. Without taking his eyes

Ryan Bracha

from him, Garner backed up to the door to the establishment and slid the dead bolt closed,

"Now. I didn't want to hurt you, believe me. I'm only here for one thing, and that's information. So, if you could stop crying for one minute, I'm going to ask you some questions, and then I'll be out of your hair, okay?"

The man said nothing. Garner slapped his face hard, bringing him back into the room, and calmly held the knife toward him.

"I said, okay?"

The man nodded.

"Good. Again, I'm not here to hurt you. Truly. If you can answer my questions I'll be gone in minutes."

Again the man nodded.

"Where is Paul Carter?"

"Ah dinnae-"

Garner reached to crunch the man's fingers again, eliciting a high pitched howl that at caught the attentions of at least four dogs in the surrounding area.

"Don't make this hard for yourself."

He allowed the man a minute to compose himself, before he asked again, this time a little firmer. The man nodded.

"Ah ken ay um, aye," he cried, "but ah dinnae ken the cunt personally. Davie Craig looks after um. He's a big superstar doon in England likes."

"Where does he live?"

"Dinnae squeeze ma fuckin' fing- Aaaaaargh!"

"I asked you not to swear."

"Man, ah'm sorry, stop squeezin' ma fingers! Ah dinnae ken where the gadge lives, ye'd have tae ask Davie Craig, he's the man ye need tae see."

It appeared that this line of questioning had taken the pair of them as far as they could go, and once again

Ben Turner is a Dead Man

led to the conclusion that Carter would not be found without the help of one David Craig, all around hard case and known psychopath, Garner wanted to sigh again, but stopped himself short. He'd done enough of it to last him a lifetime. Instead he punched the man hard in the nose, rendering him unconscious for at least the amount of time that Garner needed to make a plain cheese sandwich and exit the premises, with only one destination available to him.

CHAPTER THREE

Shake it off.

Another of the voiceless drones unlocks viewing hatch of the door after I've been thumping at it for a good few minutes, and he stares at me gormlessly, willing me to speak.

"I want to speak with Ben," I say, feeling my chest puff out slightly in defiance. The drone makes a point of staring at my breasts, which infuriates me, but I hold myself back. He makes a nonchalant look of not caring and slams the hatch closed in my face, locking it as he goes.

"You dunking fungus!" I screech as I slam my open palm against the metal of the door.

"They'll get to us when they're ready, Nat," says Monty, who's still not dragged himself out of the depression he's been sinking into. It's very unlike him. I move myself from the door and take a seat beside my friend. My fingers snake around his on his knee, and I squeeze them with what I hope is reassurance.

"You're not yourself Monty, what's wrong?" I ask, genuinely concerned.

"I don't know, Nat. My head hasn't felt right since they wrecked our car, it's probably just concussion, don't worry about me, I'll shake it off," he winks at me with those tiny eyes, and offers a thin smile. He's never looked more fragile in all of the time I've known him. I return his smile sadly.

"You're a hard man Mr McFarlane," I say.

At last they speak.

"Ben, the wee lassie sais she wants tae talk wi' ye," said Craig, entering the large subterranean room that housed two makeshift beds, each situated in their own corner. In the middle of the room was a table, with two chairs, and on a shelving unit was a box filled with technological items. Palmtop computers, non-lethal weaponry, and trackers. None of this had been fetched by Ben or his team, they had been left in a hurry by the previous occupants, with whom Ben Turner was more than just acquainted; he had been one of those occupants. He looked to Craig from his place on one of the beds.

"She say what she wanted to talk about?" he asked.

"Nup, just sais she wants to talk tae ye," replied Craig.

"Let her stew some more, she's hard enough, I guarantee it."

"Aye, but her auld boy wi' the curly mowser didnae look quite so smart, eh? Bashed his heid up pretty bad, likes."

"Send Keith to have a look at him, make sure he's okay, yeah?"

"Aye," said Craig, turning on his heels to find one of the others, and leaving Ben to his solitude once again.

Although he'd never spent a massive amount of time here, the place still held a great deal of importance in Ben's heart. It had been the place that he'd first registered that Paul Carter's potential was far greater than even the man himself could ever get over. The time he'd recorded a video designed to taunt Wilson Becker and the government. He called the country to an arms that they'd never really truly get behind, but what it did was plant a seed. It showed the people of New Britain that they could stand up and fight if they wanted to. It didn't matter how many of you there were, if your heart was completely into the idea, then you'd find a way. That was part of Ben's great pride, seeing Carter evolve from petty and desperate murderer to unlikely freedom fighter. That it was Ben's fault that they were tracked down by the very same law men they'd deigned to irritate was something of a regret of his, but in the grand scheme it worked out alright. He felt his eyes grow heavy in the midst of his reminiscence, and the warm beauty of sleep lured him like a sailor to the rocks of a deadly siren. His mind faded from thought to nothing, and that sleep dragged him-

"Ben, fur fuck's sake, come on, man!"

He was snatched from his reverie by the desperate and urgent cries from Craig, the young lad shoving him hard to wake him. His first thought was to wonder how long he'd been under, but the distressed look in Craig's eyes beat those thoughts away.

"What's up?" he asked, dragging himself upright from the bed.

"It's fuckin' Keith, man. Thon lassie's gone fuckin' mental, likes."

Ben followed the young Scot into the corridor and through to the door of the cell which housed the woman Nat Sweeney, and her moustachioed accomplice. Craig looked up to his leader with panic in his eyes, before pulling open the viewing hatch.

What you might call Catch 22.

The little hatch opens, and Bens face appears in it. I can't tell whether he's affected by what he's seeing or not, because he just looks like he's watching two dogs locked together after dunking in a park. Bemused amusement.

Ben Turner is a Dead Man

What he's seeing is me with my arms around the throat of the bearded ginger man that he's sent to check up on Monty. He'd silently come into the cell, said nothing, just squatted in front of Monty, placed both hands on his head, and begun to inspect him. Eventually he spoke, and it was then that it kicked off. He spoke in a broad Scottish accent; I couldn't tell you what he was going to say because Monty saw red. He freed his head of the man's grasp and forced his forehead down upon the bridge of his nose. The Scotsman fell back, and I saw my in. I made a grab for him and I wrapped my arms around his neck, and I squeezed. Of course the young sleazy lad who stared at my breasts made a run for it and locked the door before we could break out, and now we're in what you might call *Catch 22.*

"Let us go, Ben, and I'll spare this ginger fool's life," I say from behind the head of the aforementioned ginger fool.

"Hey, that's as good as racist, you know?" he smiles, "he can't help what colour his hair is, especially since he's Scottish."

He turns to whoever at the side of him as if to gain some sort of verification for his joke, before turning back to us.

"Hey Keith, don't worry my good man, she's gonna do fuck all."

The man's unwavering nonchalance infuriates me, so I place an extra squeeze on the throat of my quarry. His arms flail pathetically before he realises himself and he attempts to loosen my grip.

"Oh, I'm sorry," I say, "I thought *fuck all* meant strangle the fungus out of your ginger friend."

"Okay, okay. Let me put it this way instead for you then," he smiles, "you let my ginger friend go, and he'll help your old friend to live."

Ben sends my attention behind me where Monty is in the midst of a seizure. Oh God, Monty!

Not ideal at all.

Ben unlocked the door to allow Keith to stumble through it after Nat let him go so she could attend to her old friend.
"She's fuckin' radged, man," he gasped, one hand feeling against the freed skin of his strangled throat, the other dabbing tentatively against the sticky blood on his nose.
"Behave yourself, Big K, you've had worse than that mate, remember when-"
"Please, you need to help him," said the voice inside the cell, "please."
Ben turned his attention back to the trouble behind the hatch.
"Why would we do that? So you can go attacking people again?"
"I'm sorry, I'll do anything you want, just help him, please" she begged, pure desperation in her eyes. She clearly had a lot of time for the old timer. Ben sighed. Looked at Keith, who as the only man in the building with a first aid certificate, seemed the old boy's only hope. Once again Ben sighed, and opened the door, beckoning for Keith to do the necessary. Keith looked up from his place on the floor with a look of incredulity.
"Eh? Get tae fuck, son! Auld cunt broke ma fuckin' nose!" he bellowed. Ben was unmoved.
"You don't help him and I'll break the rest of your fuckin' face."
"Ye dinnae think Davie'll hear aboot this, eh?" Keith snarled back.

"I know he will, cause I'll tell him, you great big bell end. Just sort the boy out," said Ben, once again swinging an arm to welcome Keith back into the cell. "Yer a fuckin' liability, son," he whined, pulling himself upright and passing Ben on his way into the cell.

"Are you still talking? I'm bored, Keith. You're boring."

Keith turned back to look at Ben with venom as he approached the convulsing body of Monty on the floor. Nat stepped away from her friend and allowed him to do as he needed. Keith squatted over him, and firmly held his hands around the man's cheeks as he violently shook between them. Keith smiled.

"It's gonnae be awright ma man," he whispered, still holding his grip tight around Monty's face, "ye'll get through it."

The convulsions slowed before long, allowing Ben to take his eyes from the scene and lay his gaze upon the worried looking Nat. She looked back at him, and a flicker of a grateful smile struck her face. He looked back to Keith, who, still holding the head of Monty, turned back to Ben.

"There we go, eh?" he said, smiling malevolently to his boss, "right as rain," before he drove down Monty's skull against the hard concrete floor, and then again. Nat screamed, swinging her own boot hard into Keith's ginger bearded face. He didn't let go though, he continued to smash the old man's skull against the concrete. Ben acted as quickly as he could, rushing the crazed figure of Keith, throwing him across the drop-down bed and into the wall of the cell, but it was too late. The old man was dead. Approximately thirty seconds later, so was Keith, as Natalie Sweeney clamped onto his bearded throat with her teeth, and didn't stop pulling until the room was covered in the ginger Scotsman's blood, and she had been dragged from his corpse by both Ben Turner and his young associate Craig.

The list.

I watch the valley before me as the sun begins to set. The hill behind the police station rolls down in a rapidly descending sheet of greenery, making way for abandoned roads, and what looks like a shopping centre in the distance. I've been sitting here for well over an hour, and nobody has come to check I'm still here yet. I'm going nowhere while they still have my friends, and not least while they still have Monty's body. The dried blood of that parcel shelf that killed him feels tight against my skin, and I run my sleeve against it and watch the tiny weak shards fall away from me. I don't know what I might have caught from swallowing so much of his blood, especially knowing he used to run with the reported minefield of disease that is Ben Turner, but I don't care right now. They killed Monty.
"I'm sorry about your friend," says a voice, Ben, "seriously, I'm sorry. I didn't mean for that to happen."
I say nothing as he joins me on the grass, and watches the valley with me. We sit for a short time, before I speak.
"I'm not sorry about yours."
Ben sniggers, but says nothing.
"I know who you are," I say, "what you've done."
"Who am I?" he asks.
"Ben Turner," I reply, "You were with Paul Carter when he, you know?"
"I do know," he says, "I was there."

"What do you want with us? What have we done to you?"

"You want a list?"

"Yes, why not? Bullet points would work," I say, and this draws a bemused look from my captor.

"You want bullet points? Okay, how's this?" he says, pulling up a closed fist and then extending a finger as if to start a count, "One, you go around killing people," another finger comes out, "two, you go around killing people, whilst pretending to be Scottish," another finger, "three, you go around killing people whilst pretending to be Scottish and you do it all the name of my friend."

"That's all the same point-"

"And four, you go around killing people that I'm supposed to kill," he says, and I shut up, "you're fucking with the plan. They said to kill you, but I dunno, I think you've got potential."

"Potential for what?"

He says nothing for a brief moment, sucking the insides of his cheeks to chew the skin, and he looks at me.

"I think you could be what we need," he says.

"Potential for what?" I repeat.

"To help out with the next step, I think you could be the one that takes us forward," he says.

"Takes who forward?"

"People," he says, and I don't get it at all. He's being unreasonably cryptic, and just that thought alone strikes a knife of sadness into my heart. Monty.

"Can you just tell me what you're talking about?" I bark, aware that emotion is filling my tone.

"Look, I don't know why you've been doing what you have," he says, "but it's all a waste of time unless you look at the big picture."

"Which is?"

Ryan Bracha

"Because of Carter, Bobby Lodge is fucked," he says, and already I'm becoming desensitised to his casual profanity, "he's floundering, and it's up to me to make sure he can't get back up. The stupid fuckers that Davie Craig sent to help me are useless, they're a fuckin' liability, they've just proved that with what they-" he stops himself, "I want you to help me do it."

"I want to bury my friend," I say sadly as I pull myself up onto my feet, "and I want you to free the others. They've done nothing to you."

He rises beside me, and shakes his head.

"I can't do that, not yet."

"Then I'm afraid, Mr Turner, that you can go and fuck yourself."

Change of plan.

"Alright, boys?" Ben said to his assembled crew in the car park at the front of the police station. As nice as the interior of the smashed up building was, there was just a lot more space at the front. "We've got a wee change of plan, okay?"

There was grumbling between the men, most notably for Turner's casual use of the Scottish colloquialism. He didn't care that they'd rather his accent and dialect remained south of the wall, but the time spent with them and in Scotland meant that a man as absorbent of all things new as Ben Turner meant that he'd utilise theirs as often as possible. He found the Scottish accent to be on one hand abrasive and hard, but at the same time it had a musical tone to it that he couldn't resist.

"Whit kind ay a change ay plan?" asked one of them, Mark, he thought his name was. He couldn't be sure.

"We're gonna take four down at once," he said.

"Eh? How?"

"Because we're gonna kick it up a notch, my good man. That's *how*."

"Whit for?" muttered another, Martin, "whit's wrang wi' the auld plan?"

"There's nothing wrong with the old plan, it's just that we've got twice the firepower that we had before."

As he said this, Nat and her own assembled team appeared somewhat dramatically from the building. The Scots immediately bristled together, a spontaneous tensing of muscles. Various questions regarding 'the fuck' came forth. Ben held up a placatory hand.

"Seriously, listen to me, I know what we were asked to do, but believe me, when we're done Davie Craig'll have medals for each one of us. Fuck, he'll name streets after us. I promise."

The rabble calmed just slightly, but a tension remained in the air as Nat and her team approached. Her men eyeballed those of Ben's team, each with a hateful memory of the people that killed their friends.

"Look, Keith shouldn't have done what he did, and we're all sorry for that," said Ben, sweeping a hand over to generalise the apology among his team, "and Miss Sweeney was well within her rights to claim revenge for her friend. Think about how you're feeling right now for the poor stupid arsehole that was Keith. If the shoe was on the other foot you'd have done the same, right?"

Some muttering. More posturing.

"Course you would, so shut the fuck up and let's start doing what we came here to do."

Ryan Bracha

What they came here to do.

"Tough Justice! Get your hands where I can see 'em," called a voice from behind the bonnet of the van, belonging to one of three heads which bobbed up and down back there. Looking down at the prone body before her, she raised her hands. One of the heads became a full body as the first of the law men rounded the front of the van. He was tall, and thin. Snakelike. He took tentative steps toward her, a stun gun held at arm's length, directed straight at her. His two colleagues took equally measured steps behind him, a triangle of fear and apprehension. It was understandable really, given the current climate where several crew members had been killed indiscriminately in the name of Carter.

"On your knees," one of them said calmly. She did as she was bidden, lowering herself slowly to find her knees hitting the concrete in front of the body. Once she was down they appeared more confident. The front, slithering snakelike crew member straightened up somewhat, to take in the scene. Lone woman, single corpse. Crime of passion? He couldn't figure it out.

"Name?" he said, still reticent to make his move.

"I no understand," she said, her lip quivering just slightly, tears mounting above the bottom eyelids. The snake sighed. Rolled his tiny eyes. Shook his head as he looked to his colleague.

"I asked you your jackin' name," he said. She trembled as she blinked the tears down onto her pale white cheeks.

"Magda," she said, shook her head, then spoke again, "I mean, I Margaret, no Magda. Not anymore."

The snake laughed derisively, unclipped his mobile telephone, turned away from her and dialled.

Ben Turner is a Dead Man

"Yeah, no it's fine, looks a straight up murder, a stupid pretender, used to be Magda, now she's Margaret or some sherbet. Killed some bloke. The poor gherkin. Yeah. We're bringing her in. Get a room ready."

The snake ended the call, turned with a satisfied expression to the criminal, and would have told her to get up, but for the fact that she was already on her feet and had punched him hard in the throat. The snake choked, but couldn't force oxygen through his crushed wind pipe. His two colleagues would also have acted, had the corpse from the ground not suddenly and miraculously resurrected into Jacques, and then floored the pair of them in one swift movement. From nowhere they were surrounded. Jacques' corpse took the stun gun from shocked snake's hand, and jabbed it hard into the crook of his damaged neck. Squeezed down on the trigger, and forced however many volts into his body. The snake fell to the floor to join his colleagues.

Nat stood over them, firmly batting away an attempted kick, before crouching down to the offender, and drawing a blade across his throat. She repeated the action on his partner's own neck. The snake looked on in horror as two of his friends were erased from existence without a second thought. He tried in vain to drag himself away from the situation, but was pulled back by two of the girl's own team. As the blood from the dead men pooled up around them and made its way toward him he vomited onto himself. Choked back the tears.

"Please," he gargled, "please."

"I know, I know. You have children. You're just doing your job," said Nat, boredom leaking out of her like the air from a balloon. The crewmember's fear turned into confusion. Nat gasped, and held a hand to her mouth in shock horror.

"Oops. Looks like somebody's been done up like a kipper!" she laughed, reaching down to remove his telephone from his pocket, and scanning down to the last dialled number. Jacques held his hand over the snake's mouth as she called out. A man answered.

"Greg, what's up now? You sorted?"

"The *stupid pretenders* are going to take country over, we are only just begin," she said, easing back into the Eastern European accent, "send more men, and we kill also. Tell Mr Lodge that we are kill all day long." Without disconnecting she passed the mobile to Kenneth, and crouched over the snake. With one hand she pulled his tongue from out of his mouth, and with the other she drew the knife through it. The blood curdling sounds of his screams reverberated through the sky until at least as far as Nottingham.

Mr Robert Lodge adds another man to the gate.

"Green, I hope this is important, I have things to be doing."

"It is important, sir, I can assure you."

"Consider me assured, Green, spit it out."

"There have been twelve more crew members slain in the past hour."

"Twelve?"

"Yes, sir. Of four *different* crews from the northern contracts. James Finnegan has lost another three men."

"How many is that for him of late?"

"I believe he has lost eight men in the past two weeks, sir."

"Who are these people he's employing? That's what I'd like to know. We're supposed to have law enforcement on the streets that can handle it. Not crumble and die as soon as the pressure's on."

"Quite."

"Call Finnegan and tell him we have no sympathy for him. If he'd employed braver and stronger men in the first place he wouldn't find himself in such a predicament."

"But, sir."

"But what?"

"Tough Justice has lost three men, as have two of the smaller contracts. I don't believe that *who* lost the men is the point, but it is rather *who killed* those men."

"What's your point?"

"Well, sir, Tough Justice lost men to a female *pretender,* Finnegan lost men to a female No-Man's Lander. I'm not convinced that it wasn't the same person, sir. I'm not convinced that she isn't of our own country."

"What are you saying Green? That one of our own, *a girl* no less, is killing crew members? That's preposterous. Besides, who killed all of the others?"

"Perhaps cohorts? Perhaps this isn't such a small threat anymore, sir. They are growing in numbers, and it doesn't appear to be showing any signs of abating. If I'm correct, then we will see more deaths before this is over."

"I'm sure you're right, Green, but I will not bow to the threats of these people. Add another man to the gates and stop bothering me with these messages unless there is a direct threat."

"As you wish, sir."

SIX MONTHS AGO

From his vantage in the car he let his eyes wander the grounds of Davie Craig's reasonably modest abode. It was still huge by most people's standards, but compared to the fifteen bedroom, twenty bathroom mansion that Robert Lodge had acquired it was small stuff. Two men wandered around the building, one of them, the one with the bushy moustache, was gesticulating about something. It wasn't an angry way, but he seemed to be telling a story of something where he *was* angry. Garner's supposing of what that might be ended as they disappeared out of sight around the corner and toward the back. He saw his chance, and quickly clambered out of the car. He carried his secrets in their usual spot upon his back, and in his right hand he carried the knife that he'd liberated from the broken hands of the sandwich shop proprietor. In retrospect he'd felt an edge of guilt about having to do that, the man was simply defending his business, but Harry Garner was tiring of getting nowhere by being pleasant and calm. He would of course give the approach one more go with Davie Craig, but his gut told him that he would again have to get violent.

He approached the low hedge which ran the edge of the large front garden, crouching, before launching himself over the thing, and creeping to the wall of the house. After a cursory check around the corner, showing the two men still ambling along the path, a long way from getting back to the front, he edged closely along the wall to where the massive brown front door was. The warning from the man at the border -that it was unlikely that he could simply knock on the door and request an audience with the king- took centre stage in his mind as he played out his admittedly bare plan, which was to hope the door was unlocked and stealth in to wherever he needed to be, and then hope again that Davie Craig would play ball. Harry Garner lowered himself to the ground, his knee touching the gravel strip where a flower bed had maybe once navigated the walls of the house, but had been replaced out of either necessity or the laziness of never tending to the thing. His breathing slowed as he closed his eyes. He'd come a long way, and placed himself in a ridiculous amount of danger for what was essentially hope. Hope that he wasn't wasting his time. Hope that people wanted to hear his secrets. Hope that they made any sort of a difference. As he readied himself to go he was jolted from his focus by voices. English voices. Behind the door. They were approaching too. In his head the plan was falling away piece by piece and once again, it became improvisation. He simply had no time to make a getaway and reassess. Harry Garner said a silent prayer to a God he once believed in and rose from the ground, placing his back against the wall. The voices grew ever louder, until the agonising sound of the door handle releasing the bolt from the latch, and then the faint squeaks of the hinges grinding against one another. There were two men. They were from northern New Britain. Garner waited for a visual on them, desperately eager for them to miss him completely and exit his life forever.

It wasn't until the tallest of the pair strode into his line of sight and turned to lock eyeballs with him that Garner fully appreciated the enormity of this endeavour. The man's face slowly creased into confusion, his mouth forming an ever expanding letter 'O' as he attempted to say "what?" but he was halted by Garner's flailing arm, at the end of which was the twelve inch blade.

"You!" said Garner, as he stepped away from the wall and held the knife toward the pair, "you're Paul Carter."

CHAPTER FOUR

Little Miss Good Life.

I enter the room that Ben seems to have seconded for himself. There's nothing much in there, a couple of piles of rags in the corners, a table and chairs, a shelving unit. That's it. Oh, and Ben. He doesn't say anything, even when I park myself in the chair opposite him at the table. Just stares through me, deep in thought. Eventually he clicks that I'm there and he shakes his head, as if clearing away the thoughts like the shake-to-clear mechanism on an old Etch-a-Sketch toy that I remember from when I was a child.

"When did you get back?" he asks, and I find myself looking for a watch I don't own.

"Ehm, about twenty minutes ago?"

"Cool, how'd it go? Alright?"

"Yes, I think so. They think a pretender named Magda did it."

He smiles.

"You swerving the Scottish now eh?"

"Well, it was one of the four reasons you gave," I say, "I used to have a cleaner named Magda, I imagined I was her."

"A cleaner?" he says, followed by a whistle, "you lived the good life, eh?"

I find myself shifting uncomfortably in my seat the memory of what I don't have anymore.

"So tell me, little miss good life, what would a woman with a cleaner be doing murdering people for fun?"

"Revenge, I guess."

"For what?"

"For taking away what I knew. My job, my land, my life. Lodge took everything when he moved the goal posts," I say, but I'm not entirely sure why I'm opening up to him, so I leave it there. He laughs a little through his nose.

"You remind me of somebody," he says, "it doesn't do to bottle shit up. Look at me, If I think you're a dickhead I'm gonna tell you. If I may have once masturbated over a picture of you, I'm gonna tell you," he says that last part with a film of sleaze over his eyes as he throws me a wink.

"Too far, Ben," I say, ready to leave it there and go and find my friends, but he holds up his hands in mock surrender.

"Okay, okay, too far. I'm only joking, by the way. I've never done that."

"Yes you have."

"Yeah, I have, but now I know you're a revenge seeking hard ass," he says, dropping an American accent onto the last part, "I ain't gonna fuck witchu."

"Ben?" A voice comes from behind me. The young breast-starer. Ben nods and bids him to go on. "Ah'm no' sure whit we did, but there's a fuckin' riot gaun oan."

A fuckin' riot gaun oan

As they entered the room the men's eyes were all glued to the screens of the palmtop computers they held. Jacques passed one to Nat, who held it for her and Ben to view. On the screen appeared to be badly framed amateur video footage from the window of a low level of a block of flats. In the footage there were men, lots of men. Each held a picket sign, some declaring better security for crew members, others asking for lethal weapons to be supplied. A voice narrated the witness' viewpoint.

"Can you believe this? Government Authorised Crew members have gone on strike! This is Finnegan's this. They come from across the road from my house. You can't do owt wrong when they're this close, let me tell you. So anyway, I saw it on The Network to start with, they said with all of the recent murders, and then them twelve or so today, that somebody was obviously targeting them, and until they got more support from the government to keep secure, or unless they're allowed guns to make sure they're safe then they aren't doing the job, that is properly messed up stuff! What's gonna happen when people break the Guidelines? That's what I wanna know."

The footage took a sideways slant, showing a little of the narrator's bedroom. Pictures of the disabled comedian Johnny Stiff adorned the walls.

"Oi!" shouted the narrator through the muffle of the camera's microphone being bashed, "get back to work you idiots! You're supposed to be keeping us safe from rapists and people who swear! Get back to work, you jacking idiots!"

The camera then straightened up, showing the crew members offering hand gestures, with almost certainly no thumbs raised to the narrator, before it spun around to focus upon the narrator's laughing face.

"Oh man, this is mental. Proper mental."

The camera then returned to the Finnegan men holding their protests. Across from them a few people had emerged from their houses and flats to perform a closer level of surveillance with their phones, and were being shooed and shouted at by the crew members, but were ultimately left to make their videos. They were the first crew to take this action, and it had happened a lot quicker than Ben had ever hoped. He smiled at Nat, who only half returned the gesture. The list of things she'd done wrong against him was rapidly diminishing. It was because of her and her team that Finnegan's had gone as quickly as they had. All being well it would only take another couple of efforts before the country was on its knees.

We go again.

"We go again tomorrow," Ben says to me as we're walking back to his room, "we need to hit them hard and fast, you know? While the momentum's there?"
"Are you sure? Won't they be ready for us? I mean, especially whilst Finnegan are striking."
"So we double up. Strength in numbers. With Finnegan off the streets the others'll be stretched enough as it is, they can't be affording five and six guys at a time."
We reach the room, and I'm seriously doubting Ben's mental state. Not that I held much confidence in it in the first place, but his eye twitches when he's excitable and it gives me the creeps.
"Do you think it's a good idea, though? Seriously?"
"Why? What's wrong with it?"
"Nothing, I guess, it's just, I thought *I* was fucked in the head. You, you're off on another planet."
He sniggers, and a hand runs self-consciously over the shorn hair that peeks out from his skull.
"Yeah, but I'm charming. You can hide fucked-upness with charm. Nice swears, by the way. You're really getting into it, I like it."
"Thanks," I say, unsure whether Ben liking my style is what I need right now.
"The pleasure is all mine, my friend."
I shake my head at that last part.

Ben Turner is a Dead Man

"We are *not* friends," I say, instinctively folding my arms. His smile fades and now he's shaking his head in disappointment.

"Now why would you say that? We're on the same side aren't we?"

Yes, for now, I don't say. I don't say much at all for short while. The while is short, but it's long enough for Ben's eyes to narrow, and for the humour to leave his face all together. "Nat, we *are* on the same side, aren't we? What about your revenge on Lodge? I'd say that puts you right on my side."

"So what's the plan for tomorrow?" I say, doing my best to change the subject. Ben's smile returns, a knowing, sleazy smile. His thumb slowly extends upward of his fist as he nods in approval.

"Nice dodge," he says, "I think we need to spread out. There's no point focusing on just one area and the crews in it. We need to drive home that just because you ain't in Yorkshire it doesn't make you safe."

"Okay, and where do you propose we hit?"

"I propose, my plummy voiced angel, that we hit south. Straight down the M1, make it look like we're headed towards London and pick off a few on the way. We need Bobby Lodge to shit it. Make him think that he's next."

"And isn't he?" I ask, unable to slip the surprise from my voice before it leaves my body. Ben shakes his head.

"Nah, not yet. Not until phase one's done with."

"Phase one of what?"

"Don't you worry your pretty little head about that. We ain't friends, remember?"

The man infuriates me, how has he ever got through life with such an atrocious attitude? Again my arms dart up and fold themselves around one another.

"You're such a dinghy," I say, "I mean, you're a prick."

Ryan Bracha

Time to rest.

The conversation with Ben went on in much the same vein, back and forth of his misogynistic fishing and my biting every time he dipped the rod into the water, so I've taken myself off to bed to get some rest in for tomorrow. I say bed, but I'm back in a cell on a fold down board with an inch thick mattress. Ben offered a space on one of the beds in his room but I don't trust him not to try to rape me in my sleep. It would certainly only go so far as *try,* because his balls would be down his own throat before he'd even had a chance to pull his rancid member from his rancid pants. The door isn't locked, and I'm free to wander the darkened halls if I wish, but I don't. I need a respite from everything, even just for a few hours before we all rise to tackle the next part of *phase one.* The respite doesn't come, though, because every time my eyes close I see it. Monty. His head bouncing from the ground under the heavy force of the Scottish rucksack's thrusts. Monty. I can't help but feel I'm betraying him. Cavorting with Ben Turner and the idiots he calls his team.

"Don't worry about it, young lady," says the mirthful voice of Monty in the dark, "you're doing what you need to, to survive."

"But Monty," I say.

"But nothing. You said so yourself, you're in the big leagues now. There's no room for sentiment. It's kill or be killed."

Monty and Me.

I'd known him years. Since before the bomb six years ago. He was a senior partner at the law firm I worked for, McFarlane and Garner. He always had a soft spot for me, since he was a golfing buddy of my father, and he not so much fast-tracked me to Associate, but he always gave me my chance to shine, and I took it every time. When my father was killed Monty was there for me through the fall out. He'd keep my mind busy by asking for assistance with new cases all of the time. If I needed time away from it all then he would insist that I take a holiday, to go and give myself time and room to grieve. At no point at all did I ever feel patronised, or condescended to. He respected me as a lawyer, as a woman, and as a friend.

When the time came that we were called to Southwark by Harry Garner, who was Robert Lodge's second in command at the time, to tell us that the way that the law worked had changed, and we were to be put to work in far more useful industries like steel working, or mining, Monty made sure he never left my side. He saw his duty as my surrogate father to ensure my safety at all times. Harry Garner. A real dish-cloth. The glee in his eyes as he told us. He was the brother of Monty's partner in the firm, Donald Garner. When Monty was cast down and tasked with hard labour, Donald was given a comfortable number within the government, helping to make the transition from proper law and order, to the chaotic and obscene mess it has become now, as smooth as possible. He wasn't really needed, because the people jumped at the chance to take that power from our hands.

When I'd gone to him with my plan to get out of the works after Paul Carter broke the regime, Monty had simply placed his tools onto the floor, removed his Personal Protective Equipment, and hooked his arm through mine, telling me as we walked out of the doors to the factory that whatever I had planned then he trusted me, and he wanted in. Even when I had my hands wrapped around a crew member's neck, the eyes bulging to the point of exploding from their face, he stood by me. He understood why we were doing it. He understood that we needed to get out of this jacking- this *fucking* country once and for all, and he understood that this was our only way out.

In the middle of the night.

"Monty?" I say quietly into the darkness as I flicker back into consciousness. He says nothing. *Of course he says nothing, you stupid bitch, he's dead.*

I rise from my bed and blindly amble toward the door to my cell. The floor beneath me crunches as I step over the broken glass and toward a faint glow that I'm hoping is the outside.

"Ye cannae leave," a voice whispers from somewhere, before a harsh torch beam slices through the dark, it's the young breast-fan, "Ben sais ye've tae stay here. Aw youse cunts huvtae stay put"

"Tell Ben to go and fuck himself," I hiss, "I'm getting some air."

"Naw, but," he stutters.

"Naw, but nothing," I mimic, leaving the kid to hold both his dick and his torch as I exit the corridor, climbing the stairs to the ground floor.

"Ah'm comin' wi' ye then, doll," he gasps as he bounds up the stairs behind me. I sigh, and shake my head.

"Very well, but you should know, I can't think when there are Scottish *bawbags* hanging around me," I mutter. I was always very good at accents. It used to amuse my father no end.

Up the stairs and out of the building the young lad bounds tirelessly alongside me as I stride to the back of the building to my favourite spot, overlooking the valley with the abandoned shopping centre in the middle of it. I sit myself down and the Scottish kid stands by me. Looking down to me, and shining the torch directly into my eyes.

"Do you mind?" I hiss. He fumbles with the torch and clicks it off, making some half-hearted apologies, and continues to stand beside me. Unable to figure out what to do with himself.

"You either sit down and shut the fuck up, or you simply fuck off, what's it to be?"

"Ehm," he mumbles, one hand self-consciously rubbing at the back of his head.

"Look, sit down you imbecile," I say, tugging at his weak and loose hand. He's lighter than he looks, because he stumbles and falls to the ground with little to no resistance at all, before he rights himself, and sits a good metre or so from me on the grass. I feel his stare burning into my cheek, so I turn and glare at him. I'm rewarded with yet more self-consciousness as he averts his gaze. I could have fun with this but I'm simply too tired. Instead I stare across what remains of the sparkling streetlights across the valley. There aren't many left anymore. I listen to the breeze tickle through every single blade of grass, and bush on this hill. It's calming, and I even feel moved to give the idiot to my right some time. I look to see him lighting a cigarette, and to his credit he catches me looking and he offers it up. I take it from him with a quiet gratitude, and he lights another.

"So what's your name?" I ask, blowing a dart of used delicious carcinogens out into the cool night air.

"Ehm, ehm, Craig," he says nervously, like he's on a first blind date with the girl of his dreams, and he's struggling not to blow his dirty little load before he's even said hello.

"Where are you from?" I ask.

"Ehm, Bellshill," he says.

"Oh, I know it well, I have friends from there," I say, "or I *had* friends from there, it's near Glasgow isn't it?"

"Eh, aye, an' Motherwell," he says, a little more sprightly when talking about his home town.

"Yes, I used to fuck a teacher from there, friends with benefits and all that, I think he's married with kids now, but it was fun at the time," I say to a snigger from the young man beside me, "he did have weird balls though, and really small feet," I add, to a snort of mirth from Craig. He's just a kid, really. I have to wonder why he'd have anything to do with Ben.

"What are you doing here, Craig?" I ask. He shuffles uncomfortably at this.

"Ehm, gonnae take oot these English shitebags, likes," he says, battling hard not to let too much out.

"I know that, but why are you here *with Ben*?" I ask, but his face jumps several somersaults of confusion that I feel moved to elaborate, "how do you know Ben?"

Even in only the glow of the few streetlights in the distance I see his face twitching, he wants to tell me but he knows he shouldn't. I know what I do next is pretty low, even for my standards, but I do it anyway. I place my hand on his thigh, and allow my little finger to wander north only an inch. He's most certainly of the age of consent, but I still feel slightly seedy doing this. Already I can feel the material of his trousers stretching over the strain of his teenage erection. He shuffles again, his eyes closed. Still indulging in that battle in his mind. He shouldn't tell

Ben Turner is a Dead Man

me, but when my hand shifts just slightly toward his little soldier he gasps.

"Davie Craig sent us," he says, pushing himself forward, just willing my hand to reach his bits.

"I thought Davie Craig was dead? Lodge told us he died in the war?"

"Naw, man, he's never seen deid, strong as an ox, likes, he's the reason yer man Carter's livin' the dream up in En'bra," he mumbles, "c'mon, are ye gonnae wank us aff or whit? Got a stauner the size ay Big Ben, eh?"

Trust the impatience of a teenager to ruin the moment.

"No," I say, removing my hand from his thigh to a desperate and pained gasp.

"Fuck's sakes, man, that's cold as fuck, prick teasin' hoor ye," he groans.

"Watch your mouth," I warn, "how is Carter living the dream?"

I don't get anywhere near an answer, because we're joined by the omnipresent Ben Turner, who clears his throat behind us. How much he heard, I'm not sure, but you can guarantee it's enough.

"Craig," he says calmly, making the lad almost jump out of his skin, "fuck off."

The kid does as he's told and scurries off, muttering apologies between cursing my name for getting him horny.

"That was pretty naughty," says Ben as he joins me in Craig's place.

"What was?" I ask.

"Well first, you could've at least gave the kid some sort of gratification, I dunno, toss him off outside the trousers?" he chuckles, "and for second, you're digging around for information you're not entitled to."

Ryan Bracha

I don't dignify his first comment with an answer.

"Fuck you. What's happening in Scotland?"

"Right now, it's best you don't know," he says, "it'll ruin everything."

"You don't tell me and I'm leaving now, you can do your crazy plans on your own," I snap.

"You try to leave now and I'll just kill you," he says, "I don't wanna, but I will. I like you, but you have to realise who you're messing with. *What*, you're messing with."

"So tell me," I say.

"Not yet, I tell you and let you go, this all goes to shit. You stay, and you help me finish this, then I'll tell you everything. Fuck, I'll even get you out of Britain for good."

"And how are you going to do that? All of the ports are gone. Lodge had the boats destroyed."

"You serious? How realistic is it that he had every single boat in the country destroyed? You think he's some kinda King Herod for boats?" Ben hoots a forced laugh. "Okay, anyway, I know how to get off this fuckin' island, I know exactly where there's a boat, and I know when it leaves. You help me with this one little fuckin' job, and I'll take you there. Fuck, I'll even blow you a kiss as you disappear off to see the rest of the world. Until you help me though, you're getting fuck all. It'd take you forever to find it without me, so don't even think about trying anything daft. Just trust me."

SIX MONTHS AGO

Carter would be hard pressed to say he didn't recognise him. He looked rough as hell, but it was him. Harry Garner. Right hand man to one Robert Lodge.

"What do you want?" he heard his mouth asking.

"Who's this shit ticket?" Ben Turner asked, and looked to him, Carter felt his head shake to try to tell him that this was not the time, hoping that he got the message, but Ben wasn't known for his skills in subtlety, and the chances were that he was going to steam in and get himself hurt.

"Harry Garner," Carter said. Garner nodded.

"Sorry, not a fuckin' Scooby doo I'm afraid," said Ben with a shrug of the shoulders.

"Do you mind awfully not swearing?" Garner asked, as he took another step closer to the men, "it's very unbecoming."

Ben barked a laugh, stood firm but easy. His hands bunching into fists in the pockets of his jeans. A coiled spring.

"Unbecoming?" he chuckled, before dropping to perform an ironic curtsey, "my apologies, Lord *Cuntleroy*."

In less than the time it took Carter to blink Garner was on Ben and had planted the butt of the knife handle down onto his nose, dropping him to the floor, unconscious. Carter stood still, frozen stuck to the ground he was standing on, as Garner turned his attention to him.

"I didn't want to do that, but it seems everybody these days thinks it's good to swear. What's that old cliché? Swearing is the lowest form of intelligence?

Something to that effect. It shows a distinct lack of respect for the language and all that."

Carter said nothing, his eyes darting to Ben's prone body to check for signs of breathing. He seemed to be okay.

"Pick up your friend Paul, take him inside. I need to speak with you."

Without question Carter crouched to hook his hands under Ben's arms, as Garner opened the door to Davie Craig's house and entered, holding the door so Carter could drag Ben in, and then he closed the thing behind them.

"Leave him there, take me to Davie Craig."

Ben's body dropped to the ground with a heavy thud, and silently walk past Garner. Before he know it I'm in the dining room where only ten minutes ago he was enjoying breakfast. Enjoying, in as much as you can enjoy something when you're being told that somebody is out to kill you. Davie, the leader of the Scots, stood by the far window, watching something in the garden before he turned to see Carter standing, wordlessly looking at him. Trying to warn him with his eyes, but it was no use, he wasn't getting it.

"Carter, whit's gaun on, pal?" he asked curiously, to laconic silence from Carter. Davie smirked, "seriously ye cunt, open yer mooth. Yer freakin' us oot, right enough."

"Mr David Craig," Garner called out from behind Carter, he still hadn't come into the room, giving Carter a well appreciated opportunity to get out of the range of his knife arm and into the room beside a perplexed Davie, whose faced took an altogether more concerned styling.

"Ye want tae tell me whit's gaun on Paul?"

"You know the man who was looking for me?"

"Aye?"

At that Carter nodded toward Harry Garner who finally made his entrance.

"Well, my guess is, he found me."

CHAPTER FIVE

En route to Birmingham.

"Nat," says Monty from nowhere, causing me to almost jump out of my skin, and perhaps more unfortunately for Jacques, I momentarily lose control of the car and his face becomes drenched in the fizzy drink he was slurping on at the time, "if there's a boat off of Britain then as much as I hate to say it, you're going to have to work with Ben, I mean, really work."

"I know," I say, and I do. Because I can feel myself *so close* to a freedom I didn't think was possible again. I don't have to like Ben to work with him. I used to work with arseholes all the time, this is no different.

"What?" asks Gerard beside me, in Monty's seat. I shake my head.

"Nothing," I say.

In the rear view mirror I see Monty as he shifts in the seat beside Jacques, still wiping the drink from his face with his sleeve, in the back seat. I smile at Monty, who returns a moustache twirling grin.

"There's no reason for him to lie about it, is there?"

I say nothing but offer a slight shake of the head to Monty, conscious that the others will think I've lost my mind if I continue to talk to him. Maybe I *am* losing it, who knows?

"You said it yourself, though Nat. This is the big league. Be careful."

I say nothing again, just smile affectionately, and then I sigh, returning my eyes to the road.

En route to Northampton.

"Naw but, thon lassie, her fingers pure touched ma baws man, ah could huv shot ma load if Ben hadnae showed his face," Craig said enthusiastically, before taking a moment to consider what might have been, his face screwing up in disappointment, "fir fuck's sake, man."
"Yeah, good thing I did," said Ben, eyeballing the young lad with mock disdain through the rear view mirror, "you would've blown your load in more ways than one if she had," he said, turning his attention to Mark beside him, "he was *this* close to tellin' her everything."
"Naw but, naw man," Craig protested to laughter from the others, before shaking his head, muttering that they could fuck themselves.
"She's way out of your league, kid, you couldn't handle her," said Ben, "she's killed more men than you've had birthdays, nearly twice over. She's a tigress."
"Naw man, she's a wee kitten, ah'm the fuckin' tiger, eh?" Craig proclaimed loudly, thumbing his own chest. Ben shook his head and winked at the kid affectionately.
"Okay, Craig, whatever you say."

Going slightly mad.

The M1 becomes the A42 as we draw nearer to our destination. I haven't said a word to Monty since he appeared, but he remains there, in the back beside Jacques. Occasionally he'd piped up with some further doubts or pearls of wisdom but the fact of it is that he's not real. Not anymore. That hand that pulls up to his moustache to ensure that it's still waxed

tight? That's just my memory of him. His pearls of wisdom? Just my own doubts creeping in. I'm not stupid. I know what this is. I'm going jacking mad.
"What's the capital of Somalia?" I ask of the car. Jacques looks up from his phone and shrugs. Gerard mutters a question as to why I ask, which I ignore. Monty, whose geographical knowledge is second to nobody else I know, his head stays placed where it is, but his eyes reach around to look at me in the mirror. "How the blazes should I know? I'm not a bloody map," he mumbles sadly. I sigh.
"So what is it then?" Gerard asks. I shake my head. "Never mind," I say, looking to Monty with disappointment. Gerard turns his attention back to the road with a huff, and I keep driving.

The mouth of Nature's Tramp.

The car crunched slowly up the long driveway, toward the old monastery, as the light of day had fully settled in. There was crispness in the air that poured in through Ben's open window, illustrated by the faint wisps of breath coming from their mouths. "Come oan, Turner, it's brass fuckin' monkeys here, eh? Gonnae shut yer windae?" Mark asked, knowing completely that the answer would be:
"Get tae fuck."
Mark shook his head, and took a dramatic effort to rub his bald head to try to impregnate it with some warmth that would never come.
"When Craig learns how to keep his stinking bowels under control, then you can have some warmth, until then, I repeat. Get. Tae. Fuck."
"Fuckin' Nazi," Mark muttered, as Ben slowly shunted the car toward an old car park, the entrance to which had become a mess of overhanging trees from the

sky, and relentless weeds from the ground, and to
Ben he figured it was like what the mouth of nature's
tramp might look like. All twisted and grizzled
around its mouth, an unkempt beard angrily
guarding the toothless maw. The car had barely come
to halt before the Scotsmen poured from the vehicle,
desperately stamping life into their dead legs and
backsides. Ben remained seated, and pulled out his
phone.
"Yeah we're here, you ready?"

An out of body experience.

"We're here, are you ready?" Nat asked into the
mobile telephone. At the other end of the line
Kenneth mumbled to the affirmative. "Then call it in."
Nat disconnected the call, and looked to Monty beside
her. They shared a brief moment of understanding,
before turning their attention back to the building.
Beyond Monty stood Jacques. Small and powerful. A
man who had taken to the enforced manual labour
with an envious ease. Behind him was Gerard, the salt
and pepper black stubble around his hard face,
dashed with grey. A traditionally good looking kind of
bloke. He and Nat had shared a brief fling, but
nothing more. It ended on good terms, and the pair
had occasionally ventured over old ground, when the
moments arose, but never took it any further. They
knew what they were good at, and a relationship
wasn't it. Three or four minutes passed before
anything happened, but eventually the gates to the
grounds grunted open. An agonising plea to
somebody, anybody, to oil the desperate hinges. The
sound of an engine. Two engines. The noise rattled
from the surfaces of the tunnel entrance to the unit.

The light coating of hair up the back of Nat's dark neck bristled. The time was now.

Ambushed.

The vans emerged from the gated grounds of the monastery. The familiar red and black *Network Razors* logo emblazoned across the sides and tops of both of them, with the tinted windows adding further to the dark effect of the crew's branding. Through the mouth of Nature's Tramp, Ben watched them grumble slowly from their headquarters, careful not to flick any of the sharp white stones from the floor up to damage the paintwork. For a Network Crew, Ben figured they had a pretty sweet set up, other than the design flaw of that gravel path. You needed to have something smooth like a nice tarmac finish. How could you get to the scene of a crime if you were tip toeing out of your premises for fear of knackering your paint job?

"You see that?" he asked of nobody in particular, through exhaling cigarette smoke, "they're just walking into this," he said, "makin' it easy."

Nobody answered. The vans approached the mouth of the car park, and Ben flicked the ignition.

"You ready?" he asked of the three men, who responded with varying degrees of *aye*, "good, let's do it."

Ben floored the accelerator, affording himself a smile at the tasty little wheel spin before the car shot from the mouth of Nature's Tramp, screeching to a halt before the first van, which didn't need to do much by the way of making a harsh halt itself, given the snail's pace it had previously been moving at. The driver of the van peered down curiously to the car, filled with four men who didn't much look like they were planning on moving at any time soon.

Thick as custard.

Nat strode toward the first of the vans, penned in by Kenneth's stationary vehicle. The driver angrily honked the horn, before opening his door and clambering clumsily from the van.

"What the jack do you think you're doing?" he yelled, that thick as custard Brummie accent assaulting Nat's aural senses. She said nothing as she approached, "do you know who you're messing with? We're Swift Deliverers, we can have you judged, you know that?" Still she said nothing, and proceeded further with little to no caution. The crew member shook his head and balled up his fists. He was joined by three of his team, and looked back toward the second van, firstly to beckon them to join him on the frontline, and then secondly with confusion, as the driver of it struggled to get the thing into gear.

"What you doing you idiot? Get here!" he roared in as much as the accent would allow, gesticulating toward his colleague, who paid no attention. The second van jerked into gear, and lurched backwards toward the gate it had just emerged from, but to no avail. The direction was just off, and the back of the van crunched sickeningly into the corner, and becoming stuck on the hinges of the gate.

The apparent leader of the Swift Deliverers fought back the urge to swear an old time profanity, and turned his attention back to Nat. With his fists still balled he readied himself to hit her. He didn't usually like to hit women, but there was something in her eyes that said she wasn't here for an autograph-

Thud.

The apparent leader dropped to the floor, a gut wrenching pain ripping up from his beanbags into his stomach, pushing the contents up along his oesophagus and out onto the pavement with a stinking splash. She'd caught him a beauty. Nat squatted beside the crew member, yanking up his head by the greasy blond hair.

"That was disgusting, seriously," she sneered, before pulling his head up further still and drawing a knife across his throat, marvelling in the violent arc of blood which squirted through the air and came to a splattering stop at Kenneth's feet.

Like fish in a barrel.

"Get 'em then!" Ben bellowed as three of the crew members scarpered from the scene of their boss' death. The Scotsmen looked to one another, torn between releasing the crew members they had held firm, and chasing the ones who had escaped. Ben eyeballed each one venomously through the thick coating of sanguine liquid around his face. Nobody moved.

"Fuckin' idiots, man," he muttered, "hold onto them," he instructed, moving swiftly to the first van, jumping into the driver's seat and jolting the thing into life. The three men had got a good distance away, but it was eaten up in seconds as the van flattened the grass beneath it. Ben continued to curse the pansy natures of the Scotsmen as he ploughed over two of the escaping men, leaving them to try to make their escape on their bellies with at least one broken arm each. The third man had tried to make a change in direction to take him away from his friends, but it was pointless. Ben laughed maniacally as the van crunched hard over his broken body, making a comedic *whoops* comment as the lurching effort of rolling over a man's body threw him up from his seat and banged the top of his skull hard against the ceiling of the van. On his way back to the others he made extra sure of the first two men's demises, as he clicked his seat belt into place and floored the accelerator so that all four wheels of the van left the ground as he drove over their shattered bodies.

Almost done.

Only Monty stood beside Nat as she unscrewed the cap of the jerry can, and emptied the contents into the smashed open rear window of second van, still stuck hard on the hinge of the gate. The corpses of the two men from the front seats grew ever colder as the blood still dripped from the open wounds in their necks. The two men in the back screamed for mercy, begging her not to go through with it, but what they saw when they looked in her eyes wasn't human. It had no sense of mercy. It was an animal, with the smell of freedom in its nostrils. One of the men attempted an audacious escape over her shoulder but she jabbed the knife hard between his rips, and pushed his rapidly declining body back into the van. His friend made no such effort, and simply watched her as he cried his tears, made his peace with the world, and sighed. The flames consumed him quickly, along with his dying friend, and their two dead friends in the front seats. Nat walked calmly away from the van and back to her men, who saw the exact same thing as the cooked crew members. They didn't see Nat. They saw something altogether more evil. Between them they silently argued for who was returning to Sheffield in the other car.

For not more than a minute Nat surveyed the scene before her with a smile. The second van, engulfed by flames. The first van, with four dead men, slain by a single hand, scattered on the ground, each man with his own river of blood eager to escape the confines of his body, snaking off into tributaries that joined other men's rivers. *This should do it,* she thought to herself malevolently, and allowed herself a dream of the first thing she would do once she escaped this awful country.

Banished.

"You arseholes really let me down," snapped Ben, shaking his head as he climbed back into their car, "I mean you properly, really fuckin' let me down, supposed to be some of Davie Craig's best fuckin' men and you go and stand there with your fingers up your arses?"
A subdued series of excuses and apologies began, but petered out as quickly as it started. There was no point. He wouldn't be told. Ben kicked the car into gear and shunted it back along the white stone driveway, ignoring the harsh tips and taps of the paintwork being chipped. The car behind them took it a touch slower, but as it became apparent that Ben wasn't in the mood for waiting the driver, Martin, pushed the pedal a little closer to the metal, and the two cars left a slew of corpses around the former monastery to be discovered by members of their organisation.
"When we get back I think you can all fuck off back up North, if I'm gonna do it all myself with you there, what's the point of you being there?" he continued.
"Naw but-" started Craig.

"Naw but nothin', little legs, when you get back up there, I expect you to tell him exactly *why* I sent you back too, tell him you were just a bunch of pansies with a distinct lack of spine," he said, and Craig sat back in his seat. There really was no reasoning with the man when he was like this. He was an absolute lunatic.

Back in the room.

There's a silence on the drive back that I find somewhat pleasant. Monty sits beside me and says nothing. In the back seat there's nobody. Jacques and Gerard have rather sheepishly volunteered to bring the Swift Deliverers' van back with us, in case we can use it for anything. I know we don't need it for anything, and they know I know, but if they want to bring it then so be it. They've lost the bottle for it. Since Monty.

"You know they're scared of you," mutters Monty, absent-mindedly exploring his nostril with a finger.

"What makes you say that?" I ask, taking my eyes from the road just briefly to look at my dead friend.

"Oh come on, Nat. You saw the way they looked at you. You do things they'd never dream of doing. They came along for the ride, but it's proving just a little too bumpy for them. Scaredy cat rotters, the lot of them."

I let Monty's words do their thing, and it does make sense. We were supposed to be friends though. All for one, and all of that business. I'd die for any one of them. Hell, Monty's *already* died for the cause. I'm disappointed to say the least. I'll speak with them when I get back to Sheffield. We need to know where we stand. I can't work with men who are scared of me. They need to be in this one hundred per cent. Not ninety nine point nine per cent. One hundred. Together we'll fight this cause until we get that boat off of this island, and start our new lives somewhere else. If we fail then we fail together. That, in theory, is what needs to happen. In practise, however, it's going to be a hell of a lot more difficult, especially as the Swift Deliverers van carrying Gerard and Jacques, and Kenneth's car carrying the rest of them both exit the motorway at the junction behind me, and I'm not entirely convinced that they have any intentions of joining me again. Absolute harris holes.

"Well, I suppose that answers that," deadpans Monty. I suppose it does. I could follow them, argue my case, but what's the point? They needed to be in this one hundred per cent, this just proves they weren't. They're my friends, but with any luck they'll be ambushed and killed, the bandstands know too many of my secrets.

Two hours later.

I enter the old police station that has become our base alone in the early afternoon. There doesn't seem to be anybody else around, so I would presume that Ben and his team have yet to return. I descend to the subterranean level in the scant glow of the handful of electric lamps that have been dotted around the place, and head to Ben's room. I'm sure he'll not mind me having a little rest in some degree of comfort. I'm more than a little surprised when I enter his room to find him sitting alone behind the table, the subtle but recognisable blue glow of the Network emanating from the device in his hands and turning purple against the thick blood that coats his face.

"Oh," I say pulling a hand to my mouth, "I didn't think you were back."

Ben Turner is a Dead Man

"Yeah, about half an hour ago," he says without giving his full attention to me.

"Where are the rest of your team?" I ask.

"We did it," he says, ignoring my question but finally looking up to me with a smile, "we fuckin' did it!"

What we fuckin' did.

Ben tells me that in the last hour the crews we killed have been discovered, and as a result there has been an industry wide strike. There was already Finnegan's who went yesterday. Today, the Network Razors and The Swift Deliverers went first, of course, followed by Wrecking Ball, and Tough Justice. In the last ten minutes, the huge contract in London has gone too, as Tony Devine lost all of his crews to the strike. Ben swiped through each organisation's Network synopsis to show that they weren't currently accepting calls regarding crime due to industrial action. Once he'd finished with the biggies he browsed the smaller one-crew contracts. Nobody is accepting calls. Robert Lodge will have an absolute fit at this. But not as much as the public.

There are the crews all demanding better security and tools to ensure their safety, but then most of the public are calling the crews out for their blatant lack of interest in *their* safety. In a country where the Guidelines are everything, how is it supposed to run when there's nobody to enforce them? Ben switches to the News Network and on it there are hundreds of freshly uploaded images of the pickets. Most of them are slightly blurred images submitted by the public, taken as freeze framed snippets snatched from video footage. This is immense. We've done it. We're one giant leap toward my freedom.

Not even if you were the last man alive.

I pull a cigarette from the table and light it up, my hand shaking as I pull the thing from my lips and jet an arrow of smoke out into the room. I can barely contain myself. If he weren't such a prick I'd jump Ben Turner's ignorant bones here and now.

"So where are your team?" I ask from behind my trembling hand.

"Sent 'em back home, they're fuckin' useless," he says, standing up and taking the cigarette from my fingers so he can have a pull on it, "where's yours?"

"I'm sorry to say they bottled it, one hundred per cent, I lost them somewhere around Solihull," I say, shaking my head with disappointment. Ben's eyes light up.

"So, and then there were two, eh?" he says slowly and with his words dipped in insinuation, as he places the cigarette back to my lips. I laugh.

"Not even if you were the last bandstand on Earth and we needed to do it to save the human race, Ben." He feigns hurt, and holds his hand to his heart.

"Not even then? Fuck, you're a cold bitch. What if I told you I had ten inches of dangling death?"

"It could be ten inches and made of gold and I still wouldn't touch it," I retort. He laughs.

"Man, I thought we shared a moment and everything."

"Believe me, if we did, it's the only thing we'll be sharing."

He smiles, and looks to be contemplating his next move in this rather entertaining back and forth, but chooses not to.

"So how'd it go in Brum? I saw on the Network you set some of the arseholes on fire? Nice move."

"Thanks," I say, "I don't remember it, to be honest."

"You don't remember setting somebody on fire?" he asks, incredulously.

"Mmhmm, it didn't feel like me doing it," I say, to which he nods.

"Yeah, I know what you mean, good job anyway," he smiles, and moves to sit back down.

"How about you?" I ask.

"You ever play Grand Theft Auto?" he asks, moving his attention back to the device in his hands.

"No, why?"

"Well, it was *exactly* like that."

I choose not to dig deeper, and leave it there.

SIX MONTHS AGO

This wasn't ideal. Not one bit.

"Fuckin' Garner? Ye think ye can just come intae ma hoose? Wavin' a knife around like ye own the place, eh?"

The man had been ranting for little over a minute, his various questions and insults turning to white noise as Garner tried to piece together his brain enough to kick start the thing.

"Ye want tae tell me whit the fuck ye think yer gonnae achieve, eh? Ye've slithered oot ay Rab Lodge's erse tae come tackle us oan yer ain, eh? Whit's the slack cunt gonnae gi' yer for yer efforts? A wee pat oan the heid?"

Garner said nothing. Kept his eyes on Carter, but with a definite focus on Davie Craig's movements. Carter seemed calm. Kept quiet. Watched the situation play out.

"You put yer blade away son, we'll go toe tae toe for a while, see whit a big man ye are then, eh?"

Garner smiled. The threat of the violent thug. Senseless. He could drop the blade, Craig would lumber towards him and be blinded, choked and paralysed before he'd laid a single finger on his intended victim.

"Something you find funny there, pal?"

"Quite the contrary, Mr Craig," he said, "I find this whole situation distinctly without humour."

"Then take that fuckin' daft wee smile aff yer face before ah beat it aff, okay?"

"Do you want to ask Paul's friend back here what happens when you can't control your swearing, Mr Craig?"

Davie looked to Carter, who shook his head, he wanted to stay out of this. Smart man.

"Contrary to my previous actions I'm not here to hurt anybody, sincerely I'm not," he said, changing the subject. There seemed not a thing he could do about the lack of imagination that other people seemed to possess when it came to the British language. Davie Craig snorted.

"Oh aye, ye've a funny way ay showin' it, get that fuckin' blade doon an' tell me whit it is ye're wantin'. Ye're aware ay the trouble ah could cause ye, right?"

"Oh, I know exactly who you are and what you're capable of Mr Craig. My brother could attest to that. You beat him to death in twenty ten. Admittedly he was there to kill you so I won't hold it against you. War is war after all," he said coldly. Craig *had* killed his brother, that was true, but no truer than his ethos that he was fair game in the midst of combat, "my quarrel isn't with you, I assure you."

"Then, ah'll ask ye one more time. Whit, the fuck, dae ye want?"

Garner's mouthed moved to form words but he was cut off by voices. Two men entering the house, arguing over something, before yet another coarse vulgarity to convey confused surprise. The men from the garden, and they had apparently stumbled across the unconscious body of Carter's accomplice. Davie Craig's face contorted into evil satisfaction. He obviously thought he'd gained the upper hand. Harry Garner sighed. This was turning into far more trouble than it was worth with every passing minute of the day. If he allowed them to outnumber him too much they would overcome him, and doubtlessly disallow him five minutes to explain. The voices were approaching. Without taking his eyes from Carter and Craig, Garner pivoted on the balls of his heels ninety degrees to allow him vision of the corner. The sound of a voice asking after Davie Craig was closely followed by the sight of the moustached man rapidly rounding the corner. He paused to take in the scene before him, his associate tumbling into the back of him, eager to get to the bottom of the situation. Moustache had obviously been spurned into action as he leapt for Garner, who deftly dodged the approaching man, throwing a hard fist into his jaw as they passed one another, knocking him to the floor. The other man advanced, spreading his body as if to attempt to smother Garner, who regrettably was forced to slide the knife into his side, drawing a squeal of anguish as the hilt prevented it from inching deeper in. A volley of confused abuse washed over him as he ripped the knife from the man's torso and fled the scene, and the house.

CHAPTER SIX

What happened next.

- In Doncaster a man by the name of Sam Charlton was beaten to death for continually urinating against his neighbour's fence. In retaliation, the man's two teenage sons burned down the house of the neighbour an hour later, killing the entire family, including their rabbit. There has since been no retaliation, but the younger of the two sons was raped that same night by three Pretend Britons whilst on the way home from seeing a friend.

- At the same time as the house burned to the ground, Rebecca Stanley in Exeter murdered her husband and sister, she'd known for years that they'd been having an affair. After the act she went home and admitted the crime on her Network synopsis. No further action was taken.

- In London a taxi driver named Gavin McNally pulled up alongside several taxi ranks, waited until a fair was close, and then drove away screaming obscenities at them. During one of these childish acts, he accidentally mowed down an elderly gentleman. When he tried to help the victim, he was beaten to death by an angry mob, who then turned on each other. There were eight deaths.

- A riot in Manchester after a Pretend Briton was attacked and left for dead by angry scientist Marc Wayne Smith saw a further sixteen deaths in two hours, it continues now and the death toll stands at eighty four.

- A woman named Nicola Hutchinson on holiday in Blackpool dragged the cashier of an amusement arcade to the top of the tower, and cast him down onto the tiles filled with quotes from old time British comedians, because he didn't have change for Nicola's twenty pound note.

- In Southampton a man named David Owens was hunted and killed by a popular celebrity chef after the chef was targeted in one of David's comedic skits on his Network synopsis which declared amusing made-up facts to be true.

- In Rotherham a man named Liam Moore was killed by a work colleague because he had eaten that colleague's sandwiches from the communal refrigerator the previous day. In what was taken to be an ironic act, the colleague placed a sandwich in Moore's mouth, and then repeatedly slammed the door of the fridge until Moore ceased to breath. It's not known whether it was choking on the sandwich or the repeated blows to the skull that ultimately took his life.

Mr Robert Lodge takes action.

"Sir, the streets are awash with blood."
"I was hoping you might have come to inform me of something I wasn't previously aware of, Green."
"Sorry, sir."
"Have you spoken with Tony Devine?"
"Not directly, sir, no."
"And why not?"

Ben Turner is a Dead Man

"He claims to be too upset, sir."

"Too upset? He's too trucking upset?! If Mr Devine wants to witness somebody who is too upset then he needs to come and sit in my trucking office for a few minutes! Then he'll see what upset looks like! This is a mess, Green, a real mess."

"Indeed, sir."

"What of the northern contracts? Are they any nearer a conclusion?"

"No, sir. The men aren't budging. They demand lethal weaponry if they are to take back to the streets. *They need protection,* I believe is the official line on this."

"Oh, yes, and they get lethal weaponry, the people who are responsible for their colleagues' murders will take them from their weak hands and will be further armed to destroy this beautiful country. No, it can't happen, and it won't happen."

"How might we appease them, sir?"

"Appease them? They ought to feel lucky just to have a job, Green. Do they not recall how it was before? Unemployment at an all-time high, immigration out of control!"

"Should I set up a meeting with the contract leaders, sir?"

"So I can beg them to go back to work and put some sort of order back on the streets? Do you think I'm the kind of man who begs for anything, Green?"

"No, sir."

"Exactly. No, they've made their pansy beds, they can lie together like weak homosexuals at a seedy gay orgy in them. No, I'm done with the lot of them. I know *exactly* who'll take this on."

"Sir?"

"My people."

"Sir?"

"The public, you imbecile. I want a Network advertisement up in the next ten minutes. We need some new people to take up the job, and we need them quick."

"But, how will they be trained so quickly, sir?"

"You see this leather on my chair, Green?"

"Yes, sir."

"You see how it's wearing thin?"

"Yes, sir."

"Then you'll appreciate when I compare it to my patience, and your extremely poor levels of initiative are wearing it thinner, and thinner. You're paid to think and do, Green. Not ask and do. Now get out of my sight, and don't return until we have men and women queuing through Southwark eager to enlist."

"Yes, sir."

Men and women queuing up.

Six hours later from their meeting, and Rupert Green looked down at the growing throng of people eager to give their time and efforts to the cause. Mostly men, and boys, with a scattering of women here and there. His own son had called him up excitedly, begging for a chance to join a scab crew, but he'd declined the request firmly. He couldn't have his boy on the streets, not now. There was utter lawless carnage out there, and the safest place for anybody, especially Green's only boy, was behind several locked doors, with a wardrobe in front of them for good measure.

Lodge was blinkered, still under some ridiculous delusion that the country could be saved by its own people. That was so far from the truth that it hurt. They'd relied on a firm hand to keep them under control, but without giving them the idea that they were being controlled. Give them the illusion of controlling their own lives and they'd get on with it. Happy as pigs in sherbet. But rip that proverbial rug from beneath their feet and they'd panic. As soon as the crews went on strike their control was gone. They began to realise exactly how little power they actually had, and in a very short space of time. Lodge's band aid baby of an idea with the scabs would only serve to mess things up further. Of course it would. The crews were trained in various forms of combat, or intelligence, or technology. They worked because each team had ten men with strengths in different areas. They kept each other ticking. The public face of the crew would be a strong leader, a hard leader, and several men who knew how to handle themselves. Behind the scenes would be men who knew how to bypass a number of security measures to get into a criminal's Network, there would be men who knew how to control the image of the crew. How they were presented on their Network synopsis. All that bringing scabs in would do, is bring thousands of overzealous idiots who thought they could fight. A contracted crew would be a team of men who knew how the others thought. Who could anticipate any outcome. A team of scabs would be ten chefs, all fighting over who could spoil the broth first. It was a recipe for more than disaster. It was a recipe for the end of New Britain as they knew it.

Rupert Green smiled as he sighed, adjusted his tie, and left his office to command the destruction of the once great nation that he served.

In the mix, a familiar face.

He watched a father and son sparring one another across the road. The dad blocking the boy's efforts with ease, before dropping his guard intentionally to let him get a cheeky dig into the ribs. The pair of them laughed together, and they seemed happy enough to be here, waiting as family to join the ranks and bring order back to the streets. *Jackin' fools*, Grady thought. They'd be dead within hours. The law wasn't for having fun. The law was for making sure the country was safe. For putting criminals six feet under. *That* was where the actual fun was.

Grady had, until six months ago, been a prominent part of the most feared crew in the north. The Network Cutting Crew. He became Wilson Becker's right hand man, after the sad demise of their friend Banger, at the hands of Paul Carter. He was also partly to blame for everything that was happening in New Britain just now, given that he'd managed to let Carter escape after Ben Turner had caught him with a lucky head butt. After the act, and when Carter had broken his gang out of the NCC headquarters, and Wilson Becker had been executed for his part in the whole thing, which included killing two of his own men with an illegal firearm, Grady had gone on record to tell the country that Turner was a mad man, who'd turned into an absolute animal and nobody could have controlled him. Anything to divert from the fact that it was in fact Grady who'd allowed them to escape. He'd attended counselling sessions, given Network interviews whilst weeping gently at the memory of what Turner did. He allowed himself to be turned into a figure to be pitied, but all the time telling the country he'd be back soon enough, and they applauded him for his bravery. Nobody ever believed truly that he'd be back, but at the same time they gave a collective and condescending pat on the head for at least having a dream. Well, here he was, and he was looking forward to getting back in the saddle. A man like Grady should be given his own crew. He was a leader now, an experienced hand who could whip a team of scabs into shape in no time.

As he drifted back into the now, he realised that he'd been staring at a man, and that the man was staring back, with a furrowed brow, and a look of recognition in his eyes. Grady scowled, and returned to his scanning of the crowd, looking for likely candidates to join his crew. The father and son were off the list, too much by the way of potential to fall into sentiment. No, he needed cold-hearted bandstands who understood that they were here to do a job, and a good job of it.

"Excuse me," said a voice. The man he'd been staring at. Grady snorted up, and spat phlegm onto the ground, before looking back.

"What?" he growled. No matter what the public persona he'd cultivated was, he was still the most experienced, and dangerous of all the people here.

"Do I know you?" the man asked.

"I dunno, maybe your wife's got my picture on your fireplace?"

"My wife's dead," the man said, before his eyes widened, and the reason he knew Grady dropped right into place, "you, you were NCC."

"Yep," Grady grinned, "now I'm back, and if you start thinkin' about tryin' for some kinda revenge, you better think again, 'cause I'll tear you a new one, and put my trumpet right in it. The law's the law, your wife shouldna broke it."

The man shook his head wildly, holding his hands up in a surrendering manner.

"No, you did me a favour, she'd been doing the dirty with my neighbour for months," he laughed, "I only found out when he came downstairs crying about her being dead."

"Well," said Grady, an amused confusion in his features, "then you're welcome."

"Are you here with anyone?"

"Nope, me, myself and I," Grady replied.

"You mind if I team up with you? I'm scared they'll put me with some piece of sherbet who doesn't know what they're doing," the man said.

Grady sized the man up, letting his eyes roll over the broad shoulders, fat neck, and scabbed fists, before his nose curled into an appreciative sneer and he nodded.

"Yeah, why not," he said, "but you got to understand I'm the boss, right?"

"Yeah, sure, be good to learn from you," the man said, before holding out a meaty hand, "I'm Dave, by the way, mates call me Dopper."

"Grady," he said, taking the hand firmly and briefly, before dropping it and running a hand across his shaven skull, "so you do anythin' to your neighbour?"

Dopper nodded malevolently.

"Yep, I beat him to death this morning, been waiting months to do that. Besides, everybody else is doing it, I just thought *when in Rome.*"

Grady laughed, hard. He liked Dopper already.

Elsewhere, in the crowd.

"Oof, that were a good one," laughed Euan as his son landed a well-placed jab to the ribs. Nicky jumped from foot to foot excitedly as he readied another punch, but only succeeded in planting it into his dad's block, before he grunted in frustration at himself. He dropped his fists, and pointed over his dad's shoulder.

"Eh dad, who's that?" Nicky said, looking over at the building of Robert Lodge's offices. Euan dropped his

Ben Turner is a Dead Man

guard just long enough for Nicky to slam a fist into his solar plexus, knocking the wind from his guts, before jumping around, both fists pumping the air.

"Cheeky git," smiled Euan through pained gasps. His son had sold him a beauty. He ruffled the hair on his eighteen year old son's head, before dragging him into a playful head lock, and driving his knuckles back and forth across his son's skull, drawing pained laughter and pleading to stop. Eventually he did and the pair of them halted their scrapping to take in the growing crowds. Euan and Nicky had been here longer than most. When the call for people to cross the picket line Euan was ready to do it. He didn't care that he'd be called a scab, he just wanted to get back to doing what he did best. A skewed version of what he used to do, before the regime changed.

Euan had been a police officer back in the day, not a massively successful one, nor popular with the top brass. He was just a cog in a huge wheel, but he was happy doing what he did, and he was a hero to his young boy. When the law changed to what it was now, he'd applied to join crew after crew, but had been turned down. He wasn't strong enough, or fast enough, or good enough with computers. He was a jack of few trades, master of even fewer. The term might have been *willing but unable* to do the job. The thing with Euan, though, was that he had determination. He'd trained, and trained hard. Nicky would join and spot him as he pumped the weights, would count his reps. Then they'd switch places, and drop the weights down, and he'd return the favour. They would often spend hours at a time running together, working on the stamina and the cardio, and sparred until the early hours. By hook or by crook, and with hundreds of hours work, if Euan was to become anything, it would be a crew member.

Ryan Bracha

Then Paul Carter came along, and then the war came, and it seemed like he would never make real his dream. The war. The first time he and Nicky had left the family home together to fight side by side. They had been based out of Lancaster, and saw little action. It all came down the A1 and into Newcastle, with Lancaster seemingly the home of the reserves. Yet another time he'd been overlooked. When a ceasefire was called three months in, the pair of them had been left with a sour taste in their mouths. Friends and relatives had been cut down for nothing. There'd been no winners, just a lot of empty beds at home.

Now, the second time he and Nicky had left the family home together, Euan was determined that this would be the making of them.

But who's this?

The quartet cautiously approached the rear of the throng, a mass of excited chatter and noise from the assembled crowd. None of them thought this was the best idea that could have been had, but without a leader to voice anything to the contrary, they simply each went along with the plan.

"Ladies, and gentlemen," hissed a well-spoken voice through a loud speaker. The crowd hushed, heads spinning to the man calling from the balcony. He was flanked by two men dressed in green camouflage uniforms, who should probably have worn beige horizontally striped camouflage if they were ever to blend in to their brickwork surroundings.

"If I can have your attention, please," he continued, "My name is Rupert Green. I'd like to firstly express my gratitude, and that of your Prime Minister, Mr Robert Lodge."

A cheer went up at the utterance of the leader's name, fists pumped the air.

"Indeed," said Green, from the balcony, "I'd also like to thank you on behalf of your countrymen. You answered the call for assistance immediately, and I cannot think of anybody else that I'd like to have protect our streets."

Another cheer. The quartet at the back of the throng eyed one another sheepishly. They shouldn't be here and they knew it.

"Of course, our whole country needs your help, and there are hundreds, possibly thousands of positions that need to be filled beyond the picket line. If you don't wish to do it, then you are free to leave right now. Does anybody wish to leave?"

The crowd roared a unanimous no. The quartet once again eyed each other, as if willing them to make that first move. Nobody did anything.

"Okay, so as there are three territories, I will need you to segregate into the correct zone. On my right, between the fence and this lamp post, can anybody who is signing up for the southern territories please move there?"

People began to move, shuffling between one another to either get to the area, or remove themselves from it. The quartet remained unmoved.

"In the middle, here," Green held out two arms, as if to create invisible barriers, "London."

Again more shuffling. The quartet once again remained unmoved.

"And on my left, between London and the fence, can I assume that I see the northern territories?"

A cheer emitted from the left hand side of Green's position. The quartet said nothing.

"Thank you. Now, I can appreciate that some of you have come here with friends, and may wish to

operate together, and this is absolutely fine," said Green, "but I need you to be in groups of eight to ten."
Already people began sounding each other out. Knowing nods, and a chatter began to rise up.
"Quiet, please. There'll be plenty of time for talk in a moment."
A hush washed over the crowd.
"Thank you. Now, if you haven't found people to work with, then you will be put into groups by our people down there. We cannot have rogue groups of two or three wandering the country, this needs to be done correctly if we are ever to have order on our streets. Also, you need to have a leader. It will not work if you all want to play boss. If you cannot decide a leader, then once again you will have one assigned by our people."
The quartet remained unmoved, although each one of them had begun to seriously doubt the wisdom in the move. She would kill them.
"So now, as you can see there are enlisting tables below me. I need you to form orderly queues, alone or in your groups, and I need you to register. We simply cannot have ghosts wandering the streets. Once you have signed up, then you are strictly bound by The Guidelines, and you need to act accordingly. Do I make myself clear?"
Another cheer.
"Good. In that case, welcome to the first day of the rest of your lives. You make me feel proud to be British."
The quartet watched the people around them sound each other out, and make new alliances at the drop of a hat, and still they remained unmoved.
"Can I be the first to put on record that I'm not really sure that this is such a good idea?" said Jacques, flicking his gaze toward Gerard, who screwed his face

into an I-know-what-you-mean look, and then shrugged.

"We're here now," he muttered, but inside he wished he'd been the first one to make that call.

Forming alliances.

"Hey, you two!" Grady called out to the sparring father and son. The younger of whom had managed to score a little appreciation from the former crew member when he pulled the old look-at-that move on his dad before smashing him a good one in the guts. The pair looked to him.

"Yeah?"

"You wanna team up with me and Dopper?"

The pair looked at one another, shrugged, and nodded.

"Yeah, why not?"

"Nice. I'm the leader, though. You gotta understand." Both men again shrugged.

"Good, you know who I am?"

The son shook his head, but the dad nodded.

"You're Grady," he said, "you took Paul Carter on."

"That's right, now you might've seen or read some business about me bein' soft in the head. It's bullsherbet. I'll kill ya as much as look at ya, so just remember that if you start gettin' any ideas, okay?" Again the men shrugged.

"Okay. That's four. We need at least four more."

Checking the shelf out.

Euan struggled to contain the excitement in his voice when he'd spoken to Grady. Of course he knew who he was. He was one of the bandstands who'd said he wasn't good enough to join the NCC. Of course, in retrospect he was glad to have not been a part of it once Paul Carter had ripped them to bits, but the burn of rejection still stung.

Nicky looked to his dad in confusion as Grady spoke. Watched his demeanour. It was very un-Euan. The way he let the man speak to him that way. Like he was sherbet on his shoe. He didn't like it at all. He wanted to pipe up and say something, anything, to remind the bloke that he was just a man, and he could be beaten to death just like anybody else, but it wasn't the time, nor the place. Plus, the man Grady had disappeared into the crowd after instructing them to wait where they were with the big bandstand called Dopper.

Grady snaked through the crowd, silently eyeballing everybody, sizing them up as a potential crew member. A man presenting himself to suitors by cracking his knuckles and glowering menacingly. No, too into how he looked. A woman dropping to the floor to do the splits. Again, trying too hard. Four men looking like Grady, no gimmicks, no nothing, just silently assessing the people around them. Perfect. "Hey, you fellas lookin' for a crew?" he muttered as he sidled up to the tallest of the team, who frowned toward Grady, before looking toward his friends. "So, are we looking for a team or what?" he asked of the others through invisible silver spoon jammed firmly into his mouth. Grady already wished he'd kept this one to himself. He hated toffs, almost as much as he hated Ben Turner, and foreigners. Almost, but not quite.

And then there were eight.

Gerard followed the wiry sneering psycho ex-crewmember through the crowd. Behind him were

Jacques, Kenneth and Barnaby. All four of them still unsure exactly what they were doing. This was a crazy idea which snowballed at a rate that none of them had anticipated.

It started when the call went out for people to cross the picket line. Gerard had mentioned it as an idea to get into the government. As a way to get another dig in at Nat, who they had all quite spectacularly managed to screw over in one go when they dumped her after Birmingham, which itself was yet another bright spark spontaneous idea that had escalated very quickly. He saw it that they had so far assisted in killing scores of men all in the name of Nat's fudged up ideas of getting off the island, without success, and she had become a slave to her compulsion to kill, especially after Monty. Francis had kicked off in a big way and clambered from the car once they'd finally pulled up, convinced that Nat had not followed them. He stormed off down the road, screaming that they were all idiots, and he'd find his way back to Nat and help her out. Gerard wasn't proud of it, but as the van ploughed into Francis' body, he felt a relief flow through him. They all knew each other's secrets, and one pair of loose angry lips wouldn't do. They laid low for a day or two, taking turns to stand guard, or sleep in the back of the van they'd stolen, before the call for help this morning from the government, and it seemed to have offered them a point to existence again. They dumped the van at around Luton, and come to Southwark together in the car. Now they were here, following the one who let Paul Carter go, to join a crew of scabs in cleaning up the streets. It was funny how fate just wouldn't let you loose of a situation. As if it wanted you in there until its natural conclusion. Gerard began to chuckle as they pushed through the crowds of people ready to cross the picket line. The ex-crew member looked back at him for a brief moment, a perturbed look in his beady eyes. As the man introduced them to the waiting trio of misfits, he continued to chuckle, building up to a ridiculous and manic bellow of a laugh as four became eight. If he didn't laugh, Gerard would probably cry.

SIX MONTHS AGO

As the ambulance doors were closed and the moustached guy with the knife wound was taken off to wherever Garner's eyes never left the front door of the house. Eventually Carter and the sweary funny man appeared from the front door, with a heck of a lot more urgency than the first time. The man that Garner had knocked out gesticulating wildly. First pointing at Carter, then the house, then himself, and then finally off into the air. His face alive with manic glee. Carter appeared a lot more negative about whatever they were discussing, which would of course be Harry. His head shaking, hands plunged deep into his pockets, his face hinting at much more of an internal dilemma. As they reached the car, Carter stopped, turned to face his friend, halting him in his noisy venting. Shook his head once again. The friend threw his hands up in exasperation, then placed one on Carter's shoulder. Calmed himself down, and spoke. Pointed at his own nose. Carter shrugged. Raised his head to look his friend in the eye. Said something. The friend's face lit up, a wicked smile slicing across it. Both of them climbed into the car, and Carter rolled it away from Davie Craig's house.

Garner followed from as safe a distance as he could. Although Edinburgh was so very bizarrely a million times more civilised than he'd expected, there were still far fewer cars on the road than there maybe had once been, and tailing a target was difficult with not much else on the road.

The acts of violence that he'd committed at the house were regrettable, of that there was no doubt. As he'd waited for Carter to leave the house again, he'd played over the events in his head. Where it had gone wrong. His own harsh responses to vulgarity, for one. On more than one occasion recently he'd let his New British sensibilities rise to the top of the bubbling pot of emotion. He needed to accept that he wasn't *in* New Britain anymore. He couldn't continue to force those he'd expected to help to live by the rules that he'd helped to enforce south of the border. If at any point he managed to get Carter on side, he would have to bite his tongue and allow the friend to spout his truly horrific words at will. His second error had been allowing himself to be cornered in the house of a man who despised him. He should quite clearly have attempted to make contact on neutral ground, but the opportunity to speak with Carter had arisen quite unexpectedly, he seized the chance, and it was a violent and bloody mistake. He was man enough to accept that, and try to move on from it. Personally, he didn't care whether the moustached man he'd stabbed pulled through or not, but for the purposes of keeping the status as quo as possible, he'd much rather he survived.

It wasn't too long, maybe five or ten minutes later, before the car in front pulled to halt before a modest house. Garner kept his head down as he passed the car, avoiding any kind of eye contact, should Carter or his friend be curious enough as to who was driving his car. In the rear view mirror he watched as they exited the car, and headed up the path to where he assumed they lived. With the location stored to memory, Harry Garner continued along the road, round the corner, before shuddering to a standstill beside a tall concrete wall.

He could see them through the window from the thick messy bushes at the end of the garden.

Carter standing by the work top, the friend in a chair having his face tended to by a girl. He recognised her as the one that had been arrested when Carter and his *army* had broken into the law enforcement headquarters to break his cousin out. Katie something. Once they had thrown the country into total disarray the army had obviously intended to retire to no-man's land never to return. *Typical,* he thought to himself. They had selfishly caused so much mayhem and chaos in New Britain, called out Robert Lodge, forced Garner to make decisions that would eventually see him fired, and then on the run, and had the arrogance to think that they could simply walk away when *they* chose to. An anger surged into his being that he hadn't anticipated. He was here ready to ask for help from Robert Lodge's enemy, but the overriding feeling that flushed into him, was that he was here to ask for help from the very people that put him in this position in the first. He shouldn't be *asking* for help. He should be demanding, and taking whatever help he required, because the truth of it was that Paul Carter and his people *owed* Harry Garner that much. They couldn't just waltz into his life, mess it up, and then waltz back out again. Garner felt his heart become heavier. The thuds pushed blood around his veins faster and faster. His breathing deepened, and he stood straight from the bushes.

With a renewed sense of purpose, Harry Garner pulled the backpack up tight to his shoulder, strode through the garden, over the children's toys, and knocked on the kitchen window.

CHAPTER SEVEN

Lying low.

The feel of warm water cascading down my back is truly magnificent. It feels like an age since I showered properly, and this power shower is serving to dramatically chip away at the stink and blood that has become embedded into my skin. My hands are dotted black with the scum and filth that fills each and every one of my tiny pores, and the chance to rub a loofah sponge coated in the rough and abrasive exfoliating soap, across every inch of my body is one I've taken with both hands. The door's locked, to remove any chance of my unlikely cohort from bursting into the bathroom accidentally-on-purpose. Monty sits, fully clothed and amusing himself on the toilet. He's become a very comforting presence in my life, maybe even more so than when he was alive.

Since I told him about the others disappearing on me, Ben has had the quite marvellous idea of finding ourselves somewhere a little more upmarket to lay low. They know where we stayed, and I wouldn't put it past them to try to screw me over some more. Especially now I'm tied in with Ben. It gives a very appealing *two birds one stone* feeling to the situation. Maybe I'm judging them by my own filthy standards, but the sentiment remains. I know for a fact that it isn't the last I've seen of the bandstands. Bastards.

So we've found ourselves sharing a lovely house just south of Manchester, in a little village named Bollington. The occupants have long since left the place, but the electricity remains, as does this simply marvellous shower. Ben was most excited to see an old motorcycle in the garage, a Silver Bullet, he called it. I don't know. I'm not big into motor vehicles. On the shelves in the house there were photographs of the family which lived here once, and I had to flip over the ones featuring the father of the family. A bearded ginger, who bore a striking resemblance to Monty's murderer, Keith. I couldn't look at him. It brought too much reality into what I'm doing.

We found tinned food in the cupboards, and some miscellany in the freezers, and we set ourselves up nicely here. Ben has his own room, filled now, with the random boxes of things he brought from the police station. He says we can use them at some point, but the jury's out on that.

The shower continues to chip rapidly away at the animal, and as I spin the large silver handle of the shower, I feel all together more human as I step onto the bath mat, Monty averts his gaze as my naked form steps across the tiles and I face the mirrored cabinet above the sink. The door swings open to reveal various pills and plasters, and most thankfully of all, a fresh toothbrush. Don't get me wrong, I would have had to make use of one of the used ones which sit collecting dust in the pot on the sink, but let's be fair, a woman has needs, no matter how many people she's killed. I place a generous blob of paste on the brush, and go to work on my furry teeth and tongue, drawing my gag reflex into play, as the sickening gipping echoes around the bathroom.

"Seriously, must you brush your tongue so much, Nat?" asks Monty, with an amused look on his face, "that gagging is rather un-ladylike."

I'm about to respond to that cheeky dig, when there's a knock at the door.

"Yesh?" I call, through the froth of paste in my mouth.

"You gonna be long? I'm busting for a shit."

"Uckosh!" I shout, "ang clinging nateesh!"

What?"

I spit a yellow brown froth into the sink, and rinse it away, slurping up some water from the tap and spitting it away.

"I said I was cleaning my teeth," I say, "I'm nearly done."

I wrap a dressing gown around myself, and open the door to see Ben, one hand on the frame, and a sleazy look in his eye.

"Heyyyy, under all that scum you look gorgeous," he purrs.

"Fuck off, Ben. Do the shit you were bursting for," I snap, and push my way past his laughing form and into the master bedroom, to look for any kind of make-up to sort my face out, and clothes to wear.

"Hey, I was looking on the Network just now, it looks like Lodge's scab idea's gaining a bit of weight. There's a few hundred people waiting to take it on," Ben calls out from the bathroom, which he hasn't closed the door of. He grunts, and a disgusting sound of faeces hitting water bounces out of the room and into mine.

"So what next? We hit *them*?" I ask, shuffling stuff around louder to try to block out the sound of him doing his business. In a drawer I find a bra which is too big for me. My boobs were never anything to write home about, My backside, however, that's what I'm most proud of. I digress.

"Nah, we keep doing that we'll be doing it until there's nobody left to do. We need to knock it up another notch."

"How do you propose we do that?"

I put on my old stinking bra, and find a nice vest which fits just fine. I cannot bear to put on my old pants, so I dig through the lacy stuff in the drawers and put a comfortable pair of the former occupant's on, before finding a pair of jeans. I catch a glimpse of myself in the mirror, and although my hair's a mess, I do look something like human again.

"Phase two, although these scabs are fuckin' with the details, the basics are the same," he says.

"And what does that entail?" I call out, impatiently.

"Never you," he says, pausing to push another heavy ball of faeces out, "mind about that. Just keep your eyes on the prize and you'll be off this island before you can say *Ben, you're my fuckin' hero, and I want your balls on my beautiful chin*."

"Your balls and my chin are destined never to meet, I can assure you," I call out, pulling the laces tight on my boots, he laughs. I approach the bathroom to see him scrutinizing a piece of used toilet paper and then dropping it into the bowl beneath him. "Now your balls and my boot, they're much more likely to become acquainted if you don't stop with that rancid talk. Seriously, it's never going to happen."

I leave the bathroom doorway to more laughter from Ben. I swear he's just doing it to get a rise out of me. I really ought to stop biting.

Phase two.

I drop myself into the passenger side, and pull down the overhead mirror. You don't know how refreshing it is to see my face looking nice again. It was like my skin had forgotten what a proper layer of foundation felt like, my eyes feel delightfully heavy with the mascara I've applied, and the waxy tack of the lip stick around my mouth feels like heaven. Really, God knows what sort of a mess I looked like for the last week or so. And my *teeth*, feel simply marvellous. My tongue runs along the smooth and white shapes inside my mouth, offset wonderfully against the deep red lip stick I'd pilfered from whoever.

"I'd have a go if nobody was lookin'," laughs Ben as he jumps into the driver's side.

"Dream on, cowboy," I smile, slapping the overhead mirror back against the ceiling of the car and looking to my accomplice, "so where is it that we're going?"

Ben twists the key in the ignition.

"Goin' on a little stakeout," he says, shifting the car into gear and reversing it out of the drive way.

"Who are we staking out?"

"Just a somebody who can guarantee us a little Network coverage," he says.

"Coverage? What do you mean?"

"What do you think I mean?"

"It sounds like you want to blow our cover," I say, trying to keep the urgency from my voice, but failing, "how are we supposed to get off the island if everybody's looking for us?"

"We? There's only you wants off my lady, I ain't goin' anywhere, got shit to do," he says, before shaking his head, "and stop asking so many fuckin' questions, you're doin' my head in."

I silently murder him with my eyes, and this goes on for a while before he looks at me with a grin.

"That's better, you're a lot prettier when you shut the fuck up."

A little stakeout.

About forty minutes later we pull up beside a large square of overgrown greenery. An old park, left to go to sherbet by the local council, over run by tall grass and weeds. You can just make out the tops of the slide, swings, and a climbing frame in the midst of all that green. It's sad really, what's happened to our country. I wouldn't go so far as to use the old cliché of *once great*, because my experience of it was never that spectacular. My father did bleat on about how it had changed, but I'm not old enough to know anything but the bad hair and fashion of the eighties, the bad music of the nineties, and then the technology boom of the noughties, before the bomb, before the country became what it is. I've never had a Churchill moment, or known the country to rule an empire. No. My memories of this *great* Britain are the Chuckle Brothers, intolerance and an awful government for as long as I've been alive. My point is that this park to many people would represent the classical definition of a once great nation. Work it out.

"You see that house there?" Ben says finally, dragging me from my day dreaming. He's pointing at about eight terraced houses at the end of the road.

"Which one?"

"That one, third from the end, blue door," he points, and I'm sure he's winding me up.

"Left or right? Both of the third from the ends have blue doors," I ask impatiently.

"Left, for fuck's sake," he sighs.

"In that case, yes, I can see it."

"That's our boy," he says.

I want to ask again, who, he's talking about, but from the background beyond his face, four feral looking teenagers appear from the growth of the old park.

"Ben," I say, quietly for some reason, "look."

He follows my line of vision to the boys, gives them the once over, before nonchalantly turning back to me, and nodding toward the house.

"So we're just checkin' out who's in and out, what kind of activity we got goin' on."

Ryan Bracha

The four boys begin the circle the car, they don't seem to hold any weapons, but they could be concealed. One of them stands directly in front of the car, and Ben shifts his seating just a little to see around the body. Completely bypassing the threat all together.

"Are you going to tell me who lives here?" I ask of Ben, but never taking my eyes off the apparent ring leader of this gang. He's standing directly in front of the car, a grey torn hooded top over which he's wearing a dark green jacket. His eyes are sunken and tired, but behind them you can see the wickedness that just itches to be unleashed.

"No, if I tell you then you'll try and talk me out of it, and I can't be talked out of it, so just go along with it. This is phase two, remember, and there are only three fuckin' phases. You're halfway to your freedom," he says, but then sighs loudly, "this bell end is getting on my tits,"

"What shall we do about them?"

"Nothin', ideally, but they're gonna blow our cover," he says, before directing his attention to the youth, "FUCK OFF!" he shouts, waving a dismissive arm. The youth stands firm.

"Perhaps there aren't any scabs in this area yet?" Ben ignores my comment, and unbuckles his seat belt.

"Wait here," he says, pulling himself from the car and approaching the youth, who admirably tries to stand firm some more. Ben mutters some things quietly to the kid, who's now joined by his three cohorts. I feel I should probably get out and back Ben up, but before the notion has even finished crossing my mind Ben has got the ring leader by the hair and pulls him screeching into the long grass. The three cohorts stand gobsmacked, before rushing into the grass

Ben Turner is a Dead Man

themselves. A few cries, a carnal roar, and some minutes later I'm moved to climb from the car, and enter the grass. A wet meaty slapping noise combined with the rustle of the grass act as my beacon, and about fifteen metres into the greenery I encounter quite an awful sight, even by my own standards. Ben is dragging the corpse of the ring leader around by one arm, which holds a knife, and he's plunging the thing into the bodies of the three others. One of them wheezes and cries for a mercy which is unlikely to arrive today.

"I did say wait there," says Ben as he drops the lifeless body to the floor to join its friends, "you can't go all weird on me, because I did say to wait."

"Who's going to go all weird?" I ask, "if I'd stumbled across you with your dick in one of them we might have a different story."

Ben barks a loud laugh out.

"That was funny, I liked that, come on, we need to find a better spot."

Meanwhile, up in No-Man's Land.

"Davie, ehm, Mr Craig, likes," Mark half smiled, half muttered to his boss as he approached him at the dining table. The room was a modest affair, given the power which Davie Craig held. Various illustrations and paintings which all, without fail, held some variation of the Saltire. A reasonably sized oak dining table which could seat eight, maybe ten at a push. Right now it held five. Davie Craig, his ridiculous brother Roan, and the English bastards. Harry Garner, Paul Carter, and his girlfriend, Katie. Four of the five stopped, placed down their cutlery and turned to address the newcomer. Only Roan Craig continued to eat, savagely ripping the ham from the bone with his hands, and slopping the stuff deep into his mouth, orgasmically moaning as he slurped the salty fat from his fingers. He was halted briefly by a swift smack on the arm from his brother.

"Fuck's sake, Roan, gie it a rest eh?"

"Naw Davie, this is guid meat, huvtae show yer appreciation properly," said Roan, "besides, ah've the biggest case ay the munchies the now eh? Ah could eat a fuckin' horse."

Katie stifled a giggle, she was a huge fan of the dopey brother, who dove straight back into the meal, closed his eyes slowly chewed, before remembering himself, and smiling a wide grin of appreciation to the English girl. The attention reverted to Mark, who continued to battle between excitable urgency, and the fine line he might be crossing should he show Davie Craig's family any less than full respect.

"Where's Ben?" asked Paul Carter, scanning the space behind Mark, as if doing so might magically conjure up his friend.

"Still doon in England, sent us aw hame, sais he wis better aff alane, didnae need us useless cunts."

"Why? What happened?"

"He went an' teamed up wi' thon lassie ye sent us doon tae deal wi', they're a pair ay fuckin' mentalists, seriously, chicken oriental," Mark shook his head, winced at the memory of the sickening crunch of the two boys' bones shattering beneath the van wheels, "some ay the shite that boy's done, enough tae gi' ye nightmares. Nat, the burd, she pure tore in tae Keith, ripped the poor cunt's neck oot wi' her teeth."

"Why would she do that?" Davie Craig cut in, feeling his blood slowly heat up, enough to shit the top end of a thermometer up.

"Keith killed her auld pal, auld fella wi' the curly mowser, she fuckin' flipped oot man," Mark muttered,

"Ben sais he deserved it, told us aw tae just forget aboot it."

"Keith killed Monty MacFarlane?" Harry Garner asked, eyes widening at the revelation.

"Aye, smashed the auld bastard's heid in," Mark confirmed.

"Then I hate to say it, but I think your friend Ben is in some trouble," Garner addressed Carter, "Natalie Sweeney and Monty MacFarlane go back a very long way, she may have done away with poor Keith, but she's a very sly woman, she won't let it lie there, believe me."

"Ah'm strugglin' tae gie a fuck whit happens tae the boy Turner just noo," Davie said, "aw he wis supposed tae do wis head doon there an' cut Sweeney an' her cronies oot ay the picture, stop they cunts pissin' all over the Scottish name."

"Tae be fair tae the girl, she started pretendin' tae be fae Poland instead," Mark said, already wishing he'd not said it, as Davie's eyes squinted, and his fists clenched on top of the oak table. Davie's eyes closed, and his lips twitched as he muttered silent profanities to himself, before he looked directly at Mark, then nodded toward the mirror on the wall.

"Roan, get us that mirror doon would ye?"

The brother looked up from the mass of pink meat on his plate.

"Eh?"

"Gaun get us the mirror doon fae the wall."

Roan did as he was bidden, pulling a four foot mirror, the faint background of which was of course the Saltire, from the wall.

"Gies a look," Davie said. Roan ambled over and held the mirror before his brother, who scrutinised the image in front of him. One hand gently nudged his own chin first to the left, and then to the right, before giving his brother the go ahead to replace the mirror on the wall.

"See, ah didnae think so, but ye were so convincin' I had tae check," Davie said, addressing Mark again, who simply looked confused, "see, *ah* thought, that *you* thought, that *ah* looked like a gied a fuck which country she went around claimin' tae be fae. But here's the truth ay it, ah dinnae gie a fuck."

Only Roan, in a state of some inebriation, dared to laugh throughout the tense exchange, his stoned hand slapping against the wooden table top.

"Fuck me, Davie, that was funny as fuck. Plenty ay work fur the punchline, but well fuckin' worth it."

Davie gave his brother an affectionate smile, before turning to Paul Carter.

"Yer boy's on his ain noo, Paul. Ah'm no blamin' you, ye cannae speak fur Ben, yer no his keeper, but see, if his actions lead tae more fuckin' war wi' they stupid cunts doon past that wall, then ah'm gonnae hold you personally responsible fur bringin' the prick tae ma hoose. So if you think that there's any danger whatsoever ay that, then it's up tae you tae act. Him an' his fuckin' slut ay a pal have shaken up the pricks doon there enough tae send thum on strike, so if ye've any idea at aw what his next move's gonnae be, ye might want tae think aboot stoppin' it."

The boy is back in town.

As he stood outside the building that he'd spent so many happy days beating anti-British bandstands to death in, Grady felt a sadness that life had now come to this. In their heyday the Network Cutting Crew were the most feared crew in the country. The most consistent performers. They were Government Authorised Network Crew of the Year at the Gankies for three years straight. Ten brothers battling against crime. Now what was he? A scab. Sure, he was the leader of his own crew, finally, and deservedly, but he knew what the British felt about scabs. To be a crew member was a position of reverence amongst most parts of society, a scab was the lowest of the low. A parasitic worm, sucking from the misfortunate position of others who were just looking for better working conditions. *Jack 'em,* thought Grady, *they give me any grief at all, I'll rip their beanbags off and jam 'em down their jackin' necks.*

"So this is where you used to work, eh?" asked Gerard, "before, you know?"

"Yeah, I know, sherbet head, feel free to remind me at every opportunity," Grady sneered, before turning back to the building. God only knew what carnage might await them. It had quite clearly not been used for anything else in the last half a year. The edges of the window-less frames on the first floor were tinged black around the edges, smoke and fire damaged from Paul Carter's endeavours. The glass crunched down to nothing on the floor beneath their feet.

"Jack it, come on, let's do this," Grady spat, striding forward toward the building. The others followed, matching him for pace. The previous sadness he'd been feeling made way to pride, he was now running his crew, and they were hand-picked by him. From this very building, he'd make sure *his* crew, *The Network Ripping Crew* became just as feared, if not even more feared, than the Network Cutting Crew ever were.

Where angels fear to tread.

Gerard hung back just slightly, beckoning his friends to do the same, where the ex-copper and his son, and the big idiot Dopper kept up pace with the volatile self-proclaimed leader of the pack, Grady. He had no idea what they were doing here with these clowns. A former crew member who was shamed out of school by his failure to deal with one Ben Turner, a revelation which served only to confirm where Gerard's loyalties lay. Of course, he could have immediately piped up with his knowledge of Turner's location, but he didn't. He kept it to himself. At the time he wasn't sure whether it was out of some belated loyalty to Nat, or whether it was down to his own personal glory hunting. In fairness, he was still struggling to decide. Then there was the former policeman whose own failures ensured that until now had kept him out of the role of crew member, and his son, who may as well be walking around with a target on his back, given his giddy demeanour. All it would take would be one idiot to fight back and he'd be down. Gerard had watched him listening eagerly to Grady's stories of people he'd killed in the line of his duty, obviously exaggerating for dramatic effect, Grady could have pulled his beanbags out and the kid would have suckled on them like a hungry piglet, hoping to bask in the reflected glory of a bullsherbetting bandstand. Then there was Dopper. The less said about that clown the better, he was a lumbering oaf with a propensity for telling whoever would listen what he'd done to his dead wife's lover. They'd all rushed in to show their cards early on, but there was that old saying about fools rushing in where angels feared to tread. Gerard, and his friends, had remained as tight-lipped as possible. It didn't pay to reveal your hand too soon, no, there was a far better pay-off in seeing exactly what the lie of the land was before you set your hat down.

The belly of the beast.

"God, it's been too long," said Grady, his shaven head swivelling to take in his surroundings, "the justice that's been served in this buildin', it'd make your eyes water. Believe me."

"You think we could look at the judgment rooms?" asked Nicky of his dad, as if they were on a tour of some Victorian prison, or Roman castle. If there was a gift shop he'd undoubtedly be in there already, flicking through personalised key rings, looking for one which bore his own name.

"Course you can, you'll be seeing them with actual criminals in them before long, kiddo," said Euan, smiling at his son.

"Yeah you will," agreed Grady with a satisfied grin, "seriously, there ain't a rush like it. Watchin' that clock tick down and they're startin' to panic, they can see there's no way out. We used to play scissor, paper, stone to see who'd get to be the one who dished out the punishment. Or if it was your birthday you got to kill everybody. Man I loved it gettin' back round to my birthday! You don't get no blues about gettin' old when you got that to look forward to, let me tell you."

The eight of them continued further into the belly of the beast, the old NCC headquarters, Grady acting as the excited tour guide to the rest of them, pointing out what happened in one room, describing the joy he'd felt when he executed several criminals. Euan, Nicky and Dopper lapped it up, where Gerard, Barnaby, Kenneth and Jacques exchanged sighs, and rolled eyes with every exaggeration that spewed forth from Grady's mouth. None of them said as much, but they were already contemplating their second mutiny in three days.

Ryan Bracha

A good time to be a comedian.

"It's a good time to be a comedian, let me tell you," said Johnny Stiff, the country's best loved disabled funny man, sniggering toward the blinking light of his webcam, "seriously, now everybody else is at the same risk of death as me, it's a leveller. I'm in here with my quite justified fear of airborne germs, and you're out there, a quite justified fear of germs on legs. It's not just the crims though, is it? We've got a bunch of amateur crewmembers making their wildest dreams come true. For years I always wanted to play out with the other kids but there were always gonna be germs, then I wanted to be on stage, but that's worse, it's like one big giant sealed up box of bacteria, no way were my mum gonna let me do that. Now there's all this crime on the streets, I'm suddenly the luckiest man alive! No need to worry about me. No, it's a very good time to be a disabled comedian with the respiratory system of a foetus."

There it was, that build up where the audience didn't know where he was going to take it, but all the while knowing that it was all leading to the self-deprecatory punchline. He was the master of it. A lifetime of online bullying, faceless keyboard warriors telling him they wished he'd just die already. He'd wished it too, once upon a time, but when the regime changed, he built up a steady confidence in his work. He took what the bullies gave him and he made it material. He took the words from their mouths, and he turned them into a dead-on cynical view of the world, but all the while bringing it back in to involve his disabilities and ailments, beating his detractors to the proverbial punch. It had earned him a lot of respect amongst his soapbox comedian peers, and eventually the detractors became supporters, and became fans. Now he was one of the most watched and best paid entertainers in the country. In advertising revenue alone he raised upwards of eight million Network credits a year. These credits would sit mostly untouched, for Johnny Stiff was a creature of simple requirements. Clean air, clean water, and clean food. As long as he had the triumvirate of cleanliness, then he wanted for nothing more. He appreciated the luxury of his just existing more than most, and would often spend hours gratefully talking with his fans on Network forums, and live video Q&A sessions. In short, Johnny Stiff was a much loved national treasure. Which made it all the more surprising, when midway through his set, the door to his flat open to reveal two people. One was a psychotic looking man in a leather jacket which looked to be too big for him, and a short cropped head, hands covered in blood. The other was a quite astoundingly beautiful brunette woman whose eyes absorbed everything before her in the room, including the wheelchair bound comedian with the gnarled and tightly clenched hands, before confusion took over and she turned to her associate. "Johnny Stiff?" she gasped, before turning back to the comedian, "seriously? Johnny Stiff is phase two?"

Johnny Stiff is phase two.

"Really, Ben, this is low, even for you. A disabled kid?" I'm absolutely stunned, so do nothing as I watch Ben lean over behind Johnny's computer and pull out the AV cable from the camera. The comedian hasn't said anything much other than making some desperate pleas to stay away from him. Something about the germs. Ben slams his hand down onto the

Ryan Bracha

microphone, knocking the recording light off in the process.

"So what's the plan here, cowboy?" I ask, knowing full well there won't be an answer to my question.

"Shut up a minute," he says to me, before turning his attention to the comedian in the wheelchair, "turn your profile off."

Johnny does as he's told, whilst at the same time holding a sleeve to his face, trying his best to filter Ben's quite obviously nasty germs from the air he's breathing in.

"Flif, bo bum eddy floater," says Johnny through the fabric of his sleeve, "iftaberrv," he continues, "ay totter von, bub bo bum eddy floater."

"No idea what you just said," sniffs Ben, side-tracked by checking all of the other rooms in the flat for other occupants. Johnny pulls his sleeve away now that the hive of bacteria that is Ben is out of breathing distance.

"I said please don't come any closer, take what you want, just don't come any closer, it's the germs, they'll kill me," he clarifies for us.

"Not if I get there first, kid," says Ben, seemingly satisfied that we're alone with Johnny in the flat, Johnny recoils in fear, as much as his frail body will allow anyway. Ben laughs.

"Nah, I'm only fuckin' with you, if you behave nicely you'll be makin' the people laugh in no time. It's not you I need, it's your audience."

"My audience?"

"Yep. You're phase two."

The penny drops. Phase two. He's going to blow our cover to make some sort of statement to the country, probably to Robert Lodge. He's trying to be Paul Carter, but on a far bigger scale. He's not just taking on a single crew, with veiled threats to the government. He's taking probably the most famous face in the country -outside of Robert Lodge- hostage, and at the same time taking hold of the most watched Network feed there is, and he's going to, I don't know what.

"Keep an eye on germs boy," he says to me, "I need to go to the car quick."

"You *are* coming back, aren't you?" I ask suspiciously as I stand before him in the doorway to the flat. It's not beyond the realms of possibility that he's setting me up. He eyes me, before sighing with disappointment.

"Dude, I thought we were past this by now? You've seen me do a shit and everything, we're on another level now, aren't we?"

I begin a retort about the shitting thing, but it's not worth it. Instead I let the crudeness go, and consider Ben. It *does* sound on some level like Ben actually believes that what he's saying should mean something to me. I shake my head and move from the doorway, allowing a free passage outside for him, which he takes with a smile.

"Watch germs boy, I'll be two minutes."

I leave him to it and return my gaze to the comedian, who's staring at me intently, something affectionate behind his eyes.

"Ehm, just, behave, okay? You'll be fine," I say, not really sure on how to speak to him.

"Did you really watch him do sherbet?" he asks, eyes widening. I know what he's doing, he's storing material, *just in case*, he gets out of this situation alive.

"No," I say, "I did not."

True to his word Ben returns a few minutes later, this time carrying a plain black holdall that I've never

Ryan Bracha

seen before. I don't recall him putting it in the car when we set off.

"What have you got there?" I ask.

"Och, just some wee crude bombs courtesy of Mr Maguire," he says in a poor Scottish accent. Wait a minute.

"Bombs?"

"Yep," he smiles, "for phase three."

Scabbed and scarred.

The screen was black. Nothing had adorned the Johnny Stiff network synopsis screen for over ten minutes now. Not even the branded Johnny Stiff logo. His audience, for the most part, would assume that technical issues had conspired to rip the funny man from their sights. It had happened before, and would no doubt happen again in the future. It was a shame, because he'd been flowing really well today. For all of the shortfalls he had physically, his mind was sharp as a tack. One of his trademark gags was that if he'd been a pantomime character he'd be Quick Whittington. Seven or eight minutes gone, and there'd been nothing.

Then suddenly the audience were rewarded for their patience with that logo. White background, with the deep green image of the classic toilet door disabled sign, sitting in front of the microphone. A stamp style font with the words Johnny Stiff sitting over the image. The logo appeared for about thirty seconds, before making way for that familiar backdrop. Only this time, there was no Johnny Stiff before it. There was only the scruffy visage, with dirt, sweat and blood buried deep into the pores. The light of the room served to highlight the scabbed and scarred skull that reflected it through the thinning hair. The eyes were familiar to most of them, in that they'd spent hours on end watching him acting up over the years, but the face which surrounded them told of a different beast all together to the one which they'd grown accustomed to.

"Ladies and gentlemen, may I have your attention, please?" said the mouth of the face which stared out into the country from Johnny Stiff's Network transmission, "some of you will know me, some of you have never heard of me, and most of you will be absolutely *thrilled*, to be back in the audience of one Benjamin Turner."

SIX MONTHS AGO

He watched the trio of faces blinking at him from behind the window. Already doubtful that this was such a good idea, but he couldn't very well continue to find himself in violent scrapes with people who didn't understand him. He needed to know, one way or the other, whether they would help him. He watched Carter speaking with the others, couldn't make out what was being said, but he appeared to be placating the foul mouthed friend somewhat. What he could possibly be promising he couldn't begin to speculate.

Contrary to everything he'd understood about Carter, it seemed that he was a calm man. Like his actions were juxtaposed against his appearance. But perhaps that was the point? *Appearances can be deceptive.* Back at Davie Craig's house he seemed only to want to cooperate, again, entirely at odds with the public perception of the man. Carter held up a hand of reassurance to the idiot and the girl, and approached the back door. Garner stepped away from the building, one eye on the pair inside the house, and one on the door, behind which Carter appeared through the mottled glass. It was now or never.

"What do you want, Garner?" asked Carter, immediately upon opening the door, "what have we possibly got that you could want?"

"It's not what I *want*, Mr Carter, it's what I *need* from you. What you owe me."

Carter involuntarily barked an astonished laugh.

"What I owe you?" he asked, "and what, may I ask, could I possibly owe you?"

"My life. The life I had. You took it, when you and your ridiculous army decided to start your futile revolution," he said, dropping a heavily sarcastic tone to the word army.

"It was hardly a revolution, and we weren't an army, we were barely even a gang. But that's by the by. If it was so futile, how am I here, in a free country?"

"But it's not your country, is it? You couldn't free your own."

"The seeds are sown, it's only a matter of time before Lodge loses the people," Carter said, "then he'll lose the country. But that's not my concern. I have everything I want. Did you really come here to ask for help, or did you come to take shots at what I did?"

Garner began another retort, but paused to reflect, Carter had a point. He was reducing himself to point scoring, and it would get them nowhere.

"I came to ask for your help," he sighed, conceding the debate.

"Let's say I helped you," said Carter, "let's say I agreed to help, what would that look like?"

"I need access to Davie Craig, I need protection, and I need your help to take Robert Lodge down. I'm a fugitive now, just like you. I need Lodge gone so that I can go home."

"Out of the question." Carter shook his head. "Even if I could get Davie to meet with you, you stabbed one of his men, he'd have you strung up before you even got through the door."

"No he wouldn't. They're amateurs. You've seen what I can do."

It was Carter's turn to concede the issue. He stepped back. Sized up the man before him. Sighed in frustration. They were getting nowhere.

"If I take you to see him, whatever happens, will you leave us alone?"

"Yes, yes I will."

Within the hour Garner was outside the house of Davie Craig once again. Carter inside, pleading his case. He rested easily against tall fence which ran alongside the driveway, his secrets held secure on his back. He'd have to reveal something to get the Scotsman onside. Something small, with the promise of larger revelations to come. He just needed Carter to work that calming magic.

"Can ah help ye there, pal?" asked a voice behind him. Garner twisted around urgently, poised to take action if necessary. What stood before him was a bald man, sunglasses on despite the grey clouds which hung heavily over Edinburgh. On his body was a postman's outfit, and in his hand burned a cigarette which, as he approached and the stink grew stronger, revealed itself to be cannabis laced. It had been a very long time since he'd encountered that smell.

"I'm, uh, waiting for somebody," Garner said, sensing zero threat from the man.

"Waitin' fur Davie?" he asked, seemingly familiar with the master of the house, and maybe not just there to deliver glad tidings in letter form.

"In a sense, yes. Do you know him?"

"Aye, he's me brar. Ah'm Roan. You're a posh cunt, eh? Whit's ma brar daein' wi' a posh cunt?"

Garner winced, closed his eyes, counted to ten.

"Please, don't use such language, it's terribly unbecoming."

The request drew hysterical laughter from the intoxicated postman. Davie Craig's brother. The laughter subsided and he smiled dopily at Garner.

"Aye, you're probably right there, captain, it shows a lack ay imagination, so they say, ah cannae help it though eh? Us Scots are true professionals when it comes tae yon swears. D'ye want a wee toke ay the doobie? Ye seem like a jumpy dude."

Garner shook his head, and politely declined, turning back to the house to see Carter approach, an apprehensive look splashed across his face.

"He'll see you, but I'm afraid you've some apologising to do. Can you stretch to a sorry or two?"

CHAPTER EIGHT

What happened next in London.

"Sir."

"Green, what is it?"

"There's been a quite dramatic turn of events in the north."

"Again with the chugging north?"

"Yes, sir, it's-"

"I've a good mind to bring that wall down to Nottingham, seriously, those blasted bandstands in the north are nothing but trouble. Worse than Scots, that's for sure."

"Indeed, sir, but-"

"I've never met an honest northerner, do you know that? Never once have I met an honest northerner, you can see it in their shifty ferret eyes beneath their flat caps, they can't be trusted."

"I agree, sir, but really-"

"They're uncouth, unclean, and damned untrustworthy. I can't say I'd ever like to spend any time in the-"

"Sir!"

"-"

"My apologies, sir, coming here and interrupting you was really not my intention, but with respect, I have a development of the utmost of importance."

"-"

"Somebody has taken the highly popular disabled soapbox Network comedian, ehm, Johnny Stiff, hostage, and is utilising his Network channel to broadcast to the country."

"-"

Ben Turner is a Dead Man

"He has essentially hijacked one of the top three most viewed channels in the country within the last couple of minutes, and is using it to express a dim view of your leadership."

"_"

"It is Ben Turner, sir."

"_"

"The right hand man of one Paul Carter."

"_"

"Please, sir, will you say something?"

"Interrupt me again, Green, and you'll go the way of Harry Garner, and I'll have your head ripped from your shoulders before you get to weasel out of my grasp like he did. Don't you, EVER! INTERRUPT! ME! AGAIN! DO YOU HEAR?!"

"Yes, sir. Sorry, sir."

"Apology accepted. With regards to the ruffian who's stolen the invalid's broadcast, we've got a functioning law enforcement in place again now, have we not?"

"We do, sir."

"In that case just open up the contract to them all. I don't care if they're based in the south, you offer the collar up to every crew in the country, he won't get far at all will he?"

Back in the room.

"So, you're all expecting germs boy to be here, tellin' you his jokes about bein' a cripple, or not bein' able to climb stairs or some shit-"

Ben gasped, wide eyed as his hand shot to his mouth, his eyebrows slowly rising.

"Oops, I let out a swear. I'm sorry. It's not allowed. I'll try to remember that. Anyway, you'll not be seeing much more of your favourite wheelchair bound funster, because he's dead."

Ryan Bracha

Ben allowed the words to sink into the brains of the audience. The typed responses condemning him to an eternity in hell. Sad faced emoticons, several thousand OMJG (Oh My Jacking God), or FML (Fungus My Life) comments, and a million more declaring Ben a monster. This was perfect. The more he could find himself vilified the more people would watch.

"Nah, I'm just fuckin' with ya. Aw, man. Shit. Fuck. Again with the cursin', I just can't cunt-rol myself. Bobby Lodge would shit a brick if he could hear me. Can you hear me Bobby? Bobster? The big Bobby L? Anyway, take a look, your boy's still alive and well. Fuck, I even gave him a mask to protect him from *ze germs.*"

Ben spun the camera around, careful to focus on Johnny, and only Johnny, sitting there in his motorised wheelchair with his shoulders heaving as the poor bastard almost had a panic attack, wheezing through the white mask around his mouth. He spun the camera back to himself.

"Hah! You see? I'm funny too. You've tuned in for jokes, right? Well, I'm just sayin', I've got jokes too. Did you hear the one about the brainwashed fucksticks who got fat because they never left their fuckin' office chairs or sofas? That's it, that's the joke. You're your own fuckin' punch lines."

Cue much more abuse directed at Ben, almost as much vitriol for his flagrant abuse of the British language, and the use of profanity. One critic went so far as to say that the cursing offended her ears. Another pitied him for his lack of imagination. That the use of swear words only showed him to lack the kind of fibre that a true British person was made with. *Fuck 'em*, he thought, *there'll be no such thing as British when I'm done with you.*

What happened next in Sheffield.

Grady was fast gaining on the scumbag as the end of the alleyway approached. The kid had been witnessed waving his donk and beanbags at a bunch of children. He was *definitely* gonna die for this. There was nobody in the history of law enforcement as it was that hadn't been executed for their sick, filthy crimes. You just didn't wave your donk at kids. You didn't touch kids. You didn't so much as have a dirty thought about children. Or you were going down for it, and Grady was gonna make sure the first collar he got would be this one. By every metre they ran he gained by a foot. The filthy donk-waving sherbet was gasping. Crying. Of course he was. He was about to be judged by the new elite of the law enforcement world. The Network Ripping Crew. With the end of alleyway approaching, there was the sound of a ruckus. Cheering, chanting. Stamping of feet. The whimpering of his prey melted into nothing, behind the chants. The space between them had been reduced to a couple of metres, step, step, step, boom. One metre, step, step-
Chaos.
The alleyway opened up to reveal a colourful array of banners, pickets, and flags. The roar of a hundred men. The blast upon his senses momentarily stunned Grady who drew to a halt, skipping urgently on one foot to try to slow his momentum. The donk-waving bandstand melted into the crowd and away from Grady's grasp. Lucky. That's what he was. Dopper, and the quiet group of posh arch holes tumbled into the back of him in an almost comedic fashion as they finally caught up to him, knocking the wind just slightly from his lungs. In anger Grady lashed out petulantly into Dopper's huge arm.

Ryan Bracha

"You clumsy rucksack!" he whined, before turning his attention back to the crowd. The picket line, consisting entirely of soft anti-British pansies, dropping their role in laying the foundations of this great nation, just because a few of them couldn't handle a few vigilantes. They didn't deserve the honour bestowed upon them by being crew members. An idea began to bubble away beneath the surface of Grady's brain. If they couldn't collar the paedophile muddy funster, then they could get themselves a handful of anti-British scumbags instead.

"You boys want to go for a big score?" he grinned to the rest of them. Barney (Grady just couldn't bring himself to call him Barnaby. Barnaby wasn't even a *word*) looked to the others, more specifically Gerard, for some sort of verification, for his opinion. Grady really needed to have a word about that. *He* was the leader, not the pretty boy posh pringle Gerard, whose bottom lip curled under as he contemplated the suggestion before he shrugged a non-committal gesture.

"That's as good as a yes for me, come on, let's get us some anti-British-"

"Boss!" a small voice echoed along the alleyway behind them. Nicky, scurrying toward them. "Boss!" Pride bristled through Grady. Boss. Yes, *he* was the boss. Nicky approached.

"Boss, there's been a message gone out from Prime Minister Lodge."

"Okay?"

"Yeah, Ben Turner, you know? Him who was with Paul Carter when they-"

"Yeah, I know, Nicky! Christ's sake!"

"He's taken Johnny Stiff hostage. Johnny Stiff!"

"And?"

"Prime Minister Lodge has opened up the contract to every new crew in the country. He says whichever crew takes him down can have anything they want. *Anything.*"

Flum.

I really have no idea of what he's doing. He's parading himself up and down before Johnny's camera. Acting the clown, playing up to the audience, but all the while with the very real threat of violence hanging over us like snow clouds over moorland. He hasn't said anything of note, just pushing himself further and further to antagonise the people watching us. Johnny wheezes into his mask in front of me. The skinny muscle-free shoulders and back, emaciated from the years of neglect, heaving up, and down with each heavy breath he takes. Up, and down. He turns to me, desperation in his eyes. Up, and down. I close my eyes and turn away from him. I can pity him for the position he's in, but I cannot give him mercy. There's far too much at stake here. Phase two. I'm almost there. I wish Ben would tell me what the plan is. I need him to tell me how close I am to the end.
"So I heard stories that I killed a dozen men with my hands tied behind my back. I heard I did a shit on the British flag," he's saying to the camera, "that's not true," he says, "I actually did a shit on a dozen men with my hands tied behind my back, and I wiped my arse with the British flag."
Flum. Flum. Flum. Flum. Flum. Flum. Flum. Computer notifications.
Probably yet another machine gun burst of angry retorts from the keyboard army. Ben laughs.
"Okay, so let's have a look at some of your responses. There's Gareth Halliday, is that *the* Gareth Halliday?

The famous artist? Big fan of your work, by the way. Anyway, he says he wants to see me buried under a big pile of *sherbet*, and you should all wipe your *arches* on me. Come on Gareth, you're letting me down, let's see some real abuse."

The name Gareth Halliday rings a bell. I think he was made famous from some low key art based Network show out of Colchester, but I'm not sure.

"Okay, so then there's Doilan Kelsall. Doilan? Is that even a word? It sounds more like some sort of floatation device. You know? *Oh no, I'm drowning, somebody save me. It's okay, grab a hold of this Doilan!*" he's doing some stupid voice, and waving his arms around in some mock drama he's playing out in his head. It's superfluous and daft, although I have to admit he has a point. Doilan isn't a word. "So, *Doilan*, the sentient floatation device, says he wants me to take a long walk off a short cliff. Really? You don't have anything better than that? A long walk off a short cliff? Well if there's water at the bottom of that short cliff I'll be okay as long as somebody throws me a Doilan."

He's in his element here. I can't help but feel that all he is, is some failed entertainer who made the wrong decisions in life, in his quest for notoriety. Now he's maybe too far gone. He's lost that naivety that he maybe once held, and replaced it with an unwavering malevolence. Maybe that's true, but it probably isn't. It doesn't matter how you get there anyway, if it's a part of you, you'll get there. All it takes is a trigger. Take me, for example. I'm beyond redemption.

What happened next in Edinburgh.

"Paul, thanks fur comin' back," said Davie Craig, shaking Carter's hand as he crossed the threshold, followed closely by his girlfriend and the prick that was Harry Garner. Garner had managed to weasel his way into their lives after a quite violent introduction, with promises of helping to take down Robert Lodge with secrets and intelligence. Neither of which had materialised yet. Davie Craig treated the man with nothing but a suspicious tolerance, and given that Craig was the man that killed Garner's brother, the mistrust was reciprocated in a big way. It didn't matter that Garner had fought on the side of the Scots in the last pointless war. The damage was permanently, and irreparably done.

"No worries, what's up?" Carter asked.

"There's been an, ehm, wee development wi' yer boy Turner, an ah'm giein' ye a head's up, because ah respect ye, but ah'm sendin' a team doon tae put the cunt oot ay the gemme once an' fur all. He's a liability."

"Development?"

"Aye, development. The bastart's goan an' kidnapped a wee spazzy kid, some famous comedian they huv doon there, a Johnny Stiff?"

"Kidnapped? In what way? Like asking for a ransom?"

"Naw, there's nae ransom, he's taken over the wee cunt's telly show, an' he's actin' the big prick fae the kid's livin' room. Fuck knows what he's plannin', but ye c'n guarantee it's designed fur an audience. Aw it's gonnae take is one wrong word fae Turner, an' we're either ower run by crazed English lookin' fur a new place tae live, or we're ower run by Rab Lodge's wee armies again, an' ah dinnae want that, despite what youse English think, ah jist want the quiet life fur ma people."

Davie let the words sink in with Carter. He felt bad for the bloke. As much as he wanted the quiet life for his people, Carter wanted the quiet life for *his* people

Ryan Bracha

too. His girlfriend, and the small family he brought with him. It wasn't his fault that Turner had gone rogue for whatever reason, but Davie's original statement still stood, it *was* Carter that brought the maniac over the border, and as such he would be held accountable for the man's actions.

"So when do your men leave?" Carter asked, after a short moment of contemplation.

"They'll head doon tonight."

"Okay. Can you do me a favour?"

"Aye, although ah suppose it depends what it is."

"I'd like a few hours head start. If your people get there and I've failed to contain it then I'll accept that you'll do whatever you need to. But I'd like the chance to sort it."

"Seriously? Ye still want tae help the cunt after aw this?"

"Davie, he's my friend, I might have brought him to Scotland, but if it wasn't for him then *none* of us would be here, if I just stand by and watch you do what you're going to do then what kind of friend am I?"

Davie eyes twinkled with respect for the man as he smiled.

"Yer a good bloke, Carter, ah dinnae gie a fuck whit anybody else sais aboot ye."

"What anybody else-"

Carter started, before realising quickly that he was on the receiving end of a Davie Craig wind-up.

"You cheeky bastard," he smiled.

"Dinnae let it be said that Davie Craig disnae have a sense ay humour. Ah'll gie ye six hours, Paul, but ah cannae let sentiment get in the way ay lookin' after ma people, okay?"

"Okay."

The men shook hands firmly, a look of resignation glimmered across Carter's face. He was being dragged back into a fight that was no longer his, but he had his principles, and he'd never forgive himself if he stood by and did nothing.

I'm coming too.

"I'm coming too, Paul Carter," said Katie, finally, after a silent journey back to their house. The three of them, Carter, Garner and Katie, each in their own bubbles of contemplation for the duration of the trip. "Do I have a choice in the matter?" Paul asked, well aware that he didn't.

"Nope," she said. Conversation over.

Garner continued to say nothing in the back. He had no intentions of going down there, not for the incessant foul mouth that was Ben Turner anyway. He'd got a plan, and it didn't involve risking everything he'd constructed for the sake of Turner. Climbing from the car he followed the others to the house, one which he'd been allowed to use of with the others. It didn't ever feel like home, just a place he slept in, between going up to the highlands for weeks at a time to train alone, and to the local bar for hours at a time to drink alone. Although he'd found himself in a place where there was an unsettled quiet between them all, he'd never found himself as a friend to any of them. He couldn't be. He'd worked with Robert Lodge to overthrow the previous government. He'd worked with Robert Lodge to create New Britain. He was a driving force behind the country which killed Katie's parents, a man who had helped, but ultimately failed, to bring Paul Carter to justice, and he had attacked Ben Turner within his first few hours of being in the country. His only saving grace at all was that he was a turncoat against Lodge, and a man of principle. He had his secrets, of course he did, and they were valuable with it, but they were for the right time. It didn't do to peak too soon.

"Will you call Maguire?" Katie asked of Carter as they entered the kitchen, leaving Garner to his own devices. Carter muttered something about not needing him, or his expertise. That it wasn't that kind of trip. Katie doubted the wisdom, and then the conversation disappeared from earshot as Garner ascended the stairs, and again up the steps to his room in the loft. It was a decent sized room, but of course being directly beneath the roof rendered a lot of the floor space useless. From his room he heard the other two climb the stairs, Katie still going on about Maguire, a chemistry teacher who'd been called upon for his skills in creating explosives once upon a time. He didn't mind Katie, in that she had character. She was a livewire with a sparkle in her eyes, and a cheeky and mischievous streak that put Ben Turner's spite and facetiousness to shame. She still, for the most part, used alternatives to cursing, instead of leaping head first into murdering the English language like the Scots, or Ben Turner, which endeared him to her. They shuffled about on the level beneath him, as he lowered himself to his bed, which was a thick mattress on the floor. He didn't need luxuries anymore. He'd lived that life, and although it was fine at the time, his last six months in this country had showed him that sometimes the simpler things were preferable.

From the comfort of his mattress, Harry Garner considered what Turner could be up to, what could he possibly think he could achieve taking Johnny Stiff hostage? What did he have to say that needed such an audience? And what of Nat Sweeney? Where did she factor in this? She'd not been mentioned by Davie Craig, so could they now assume that she'd outlived her usefulness and he'd done away with her? Quietly, Garner hoped so. She was a potentially poisonous thorn in their sides, but more especially, his.

With Nat Sweeney, Monty MacFarlane, and the law agency they represented with Donald Garner in mind, Harry reached under the mattress to retrieve his secrets. To replay every shameful act of he and Robert Lodge's time in each other's acquaintanceship, not just from the last six years of New Britain, but from long, long before that. It was the book in which he'd catalogued every nefarious deed they'd undertaken, locked away from his new found capacity for regret. It was his insurance, that should he ever find himself imprisoned, or worse, that if he was going down, he'd make damn sure that Lodge went with him. A cursory sweep beneath the mattress yielded nothing. A second, deeper delve resulted in the same. Garner felt a shortness of breath, akin to once upon a time when one might briefly experience a moment of panic when it seemed one might have lost a wallet, or mobile telephone. This time though, the moment extended long beyond brief, as he stood from the mattress, dragged it upright and pushed it away. The secrets weren't there. He ripped open the loose door of the bedside cabinet. Nothing. He pulled the few clothes which hung in the combination wardrobe, dragged the drawers from the unit. Nothing. Harry Garner's eyes flickered shut, his heart smashed against his ribs, his lungs refused him breath. His secrets were gone, and in a sickening moment of clarity, he knew exactly where they'd gone, who'd taken them, and what kind of things Ben Turner needed an audience for. He bolted from the room in a blur, his feet rattled against the steps as he descended to the first floor, and between heavy and urgent breaths, Harry Garner rounded the corner to the bedroom, tearing Paul and Katie from an embrace.

"Garner? What's up?" Carter asked, a flush of red in his cheeks with the apparent embarrassment at being caught in the act with his girlfriend. Katie simply giggled, and pushed down against his erection which harassed her leg.

"I'm coming too," he said, before leaving the lovers to it, and to pour a triple shot of whiskey. And then another.

SIX MONTHS AGO

Garner watched Davie Craig twitch in fury at his very presence in the room. How easy it would be to walk over and wring his neck. Ingratiate himself with Lodge, rather than take him down. But it wouldn't guarantee him anything. Lodge would probably rip him to pieces for doing anything without his prior permission. He was the one person by whom asking for forgiveness was treated with exactly the same amount of contempt as asking for permission.

"Paul sais ye've come tae apologise fur ye quite violent introduction earlier?" Davie Craig said, eyebrows raised as he glared at the Englishman. Garner cleared his throat. Wanted to say the words he'd silently practised as he walked into the house but they stuck there. No amount of clearing could draw them from his throat. An uneasy quiet rippled through the room.

"Paul," Davie said, addressing Carter in the corner, "ye sais he wis gonnae apologise, ah'm hearin' nowt here."

"He said he would," muttered Carter, switching is own expectant gaze to Garner, whose eyes closed, as he worked to regulate his breathing. *Suck it up.*

"Mr Craig," Garner said finally, "please accept my sincerest of apologies for my recent behaviour in your abode. My intentions were not violent when I came to your country, but I was backed into a corner and I had no choice. Although this was the case, I accept the responsibility, and I give you my word that if you grant me an audience, it will not happen again. Please pass on my apologies also, to your employee. I sincerely hope that he makes a full recovery."

Davie Craig eyeballed Garner, gauging the sincerity with which he spoke. He exhaled sharply.

"Paul also tells me ye've information to share regardin' Rab Lodge, whit information might that be?"

It was now Garner's turn to twitch in irritation. The lumbering idiot had completely bypassed the apology.

"I'll share no information with a man who has yet to accept my apologies. My *sincerest*, of apologies."

"Yer a strange fruit, Garner, a very strange fruit."

"That may be so, but the ball is in your court, Mr Craig."

Davie rubbed his thick fingers along the length of his brow, and closed his eyes. The table tennis match of petty bickering was slicing a knife tentatively across every one of his nerves.

"Right, apology accepted, let's move oan eh? Tell me whit it is that ye know aboot Rab Lodge, an' whit it is that's gonnae make a difference tae proceedins here. Pretty please, before ye start at me aboot ma P's and Q's."

Garner sat back. Once that initial breakthrough had been made it became easier. Of course, both men remained untrusting of the other. The promise of dirt on Lodge had piqued Davie enough to allow this audience, but not before he'd made Garner jump through hoops of humiliation. It was a small, and brief price to pay for the security that came with residing beneath his wing. Now it was simply a case of drip feeding him the information that would keep Garner there.

"I've known Robert since we were about eighteen. We'd enlisted in the British Army at the same time, in nineteen seventy eight. We'd served together for four years, before Thatcher's war against the Argies in eighty two. It was a short but sweet experience, but it gave us a taste for conflict, and for defending our country and her honour. We took to it like ducks to a violent water. That we'd risked our lives to protect our country's interests made it taste all the more sweet. We *were* Britain."

Garner felt a pride rise within him as he remembered the early days, slamming a fist onto the table before his to emphasise the point.

"This aw sounds like a wonderful story, but ah hope yer no gaunnae deny us the abridged version just now, Garner. Skip us forward a wee bit eh? Like whit the fuck kinda dirt de ye have oan Rab Lodge?" Davie interrupted, sensing a good point to call it.

Garner groaned quietly. Pinched the bridge of his nose. Rubbed his eyes.

"I have thirty seven years' worth of dirt, David. I didn't intend to take you on thirty seven years' worth of walking down memory lane, I was merely illustrating the kind of person Lodge was, the kind of person he is. He's fiercely nationalistic. He won't ever accept a threat to our nation. And in order to achieve the Britain of his vision, he has committed not just the atrocities that you're well aware of, but also a great many that you aren't. For starters, he had an influential pro-immigration figure murdered, and he commenced a smear campaign against the man. He was a friend of-"

"Mr Craig!" came a wonderfully timed voice from the hallway. An urgent plea for attention. A tall bearded ginger man rounded the corner with haste, a look of desperation in his eyes.

"Keith?"

"You need to come tae the comms shed quick, we've got word fae the boys in Durham that Rab Lodge has declared war."

Ryan Bracha

CHAPTER NINE

Revelations.

"People of New Britain. People of America. People of the rest of the *civilised* world," Ben said theatrically, and winked mischievously, "I hold here, a book. It's not exactly *the* book of revelations, but it's *a* book of revelations."
This was the first time I'd seen the book. I had no idea what it held, or what significance it held to our lives, at least, not at that point. It was a basic, hard backed and leather bound, brown book. Along the spine was some word, which I couldn't make out. Beside me Johnny was in a bad way. It could only have been a matter of time before he perished, either from anxiety, or from the airborne disease which threatened to destroy him at any time. I could feel my mind detaching. This was too much. *She* wasn't too far away. Ready to take me over.
"In approximately two hours I'm gonna make my first revelation. Seriously, you need to stick around for it," he said, "anybody that wants to know what Bobby Lodge gets up to when he's lurking in the shadows of your life. Anybody that wants to know how this fucked up country got the way it did, who allowed *certain things* to happen against the better judgment of others. If you want answers. Then I'd suggest you go and make yourself a brew, or get a beer, somethin' like that. Then come and get comfortable, because this is explosive stuff. Two hours. Your time, starts, now!"
Ben then flicked off the audio visual recorders and turned to Johnny and I with a grin.

"What did you think to that?" he asked of me. I didn't know what to say. I didn't say anything other than to ask him to come into the kitchen with me.

"Do you want to tell me what's going on?" I demanded, the stony glare in my eye that said I wasn't kidding. I'd been dragged along for nothing. Ben acted the big fucking idiot for the cameras, spoke in riddles and dangled a leather bound carrot for the people of the country, and I was no less of a bystander than the rest of them. Ben rolled his eyes with a smile, like he was bored of this by now. I shook my head, this wasn't the time for playing up. I was serious.

"You really want to know?"

"Of course I do. I've had enough of blindly going along with your messed up schemes, and phases. I don't care what you know or don't know about getting out of this country in the future. I want to know what's happening *now*."

He looked at me, and he held the book up.

"You know what this is?" he asked me, the question obviously rhetorical given that I'd never seen it in my entire life. I shrugged.

"This is our ticket out of here. I mean, our real ticket. Not just me and you, not just germs boy out there. Everybody."

"There you go again with being cryptic, stop being dramatic and just tell me what it is, or I'm out of here. I'll leave you and *germs boy* to your party, and I'll do my own thing. I've had enough of being your bloody sock puppet."

"Hey," he said, his face taking on a hurt demeanour, "you were never my sock puppet. Really," he said, "I thought we were gonna do this together."

"Don't change the subject," I said, I was wise to his tricks by then, "what's in the book."

Ryan Bracha

He sighed.

"Okay. But you need to promise not to freak out, because it won't help. For this to work we need to focus."

"Just fucking tell me Ben."

"It's a diary," he said with a sigh, "Harry Garner's diary."

"Harry Garner, as in, of Robert Lodge and Harry Garner overthrow the government fame?"

"The very same."

"How the hell have you got that?"

"It's a long story, but let's say he's the one who put us on to you, and let's say you feature in this book. You and Montgomery MacFarlane, which I'm assuming is your pal Monty. And somebody I'm gonna have to guess is your dad. Bartholomew Sweeney?"

I made a snatch for the book, but he saw it coming and held it out of my reach.

"No," he said, "let's just do this my way, I've got them all worked up, they'll be back in a while for something. I want to start small, and work up to the big stuff. I promise you can have the whole book when we're through. Call it your bedtime reading for when you're on the overnight ferry from Cairnryan."

Ferry. Cairnryan.

"Cairnryan? As it Scotland?"

"Yep. That's where it leaves from, for Ireland, every Friday night. See, I didn't have to tell you that, but I need you to trust me now. I've been a prick, I know I have, I *am* a prick, that's just how I roll, you can't change me and don't pretend like it doesn't turn you on like fuck," he said. He really was a misogynistic arsehole.

"Like fuck it does-"

"But we can work through our obvious attraction for each other, and make this work. So you have a choice now. You know where the ferry leaves from, you know when it leaves, and it was me that gave you that information, because I need you to trust me. You can leave me now, to probably fuck it all up without you, to get on that ferry and get the fuck off this island once and for all. Or you can see this through with me, and we can get *everybody* off this fuckin' piece of shit land, by putting a fuck off great big hole in not just Bobby Lodge's plans, but Harry fuckin' Garner, and all the other pieces of shit they conspired with."

"What did they do to my father?" I asked, a glassy view of the world balling up in my eyes, as my hands balled up into fists, and I smashed the right one into the buzzing refrigerator, "what the fuck did they do to my father?!"

"I'll tell you everything you need, Nat, just give me two hours."

He stares right at me, into my eyes. A look I've never seen from him before. Like he's a real person and not just some flapjack who can't take anything seriously. It won't last.

"You've waited this long, Nat," Monty says to me from behind Ben. I thought I'd managed to shake him off. Evidently not. Ben's staring at me and I'm staring sadly at Monty, who smiles with a warmth that reaches his eyes. I need to know, but Monty's right. I've waited this long.

Just keep quiet.

The van rumbled over Woodhead Pass. An uncomfortable silence had grown inside it since they left Sheffield, and a Network signal. Grady's instructions had been to drop everything for this job. Gerard had had to stifle a laugh when Grady had declared that *This time, it's personal.* The man really was a top shelf fool. A cartoonish caricature of everything they'd assumed the crewmembers were, before their first-hand experience with this one. Everything he said was tainted with cliché, as if he acted exactly like he thought an old school film villain should. Gerard wondered what actually went on in his head. Did he consciously decide to spit these things in the hope that they sounded menacing? Or was he really this clichéd?

When the young chap, Nicky, had come excitedly bounding along to tell them the news of Turner holding the comedian hostage, and the subsequent revelation of the open contract on his head, Gerard felt his stomach turn, as the screw turned further on them, but the more he discovered about the situation, the less concerned he was. There had been no news of Nat, or any hint that she was involved at all. They'd dropped her like a hot coal because of her increasingly violent actions, and Gerard's biggest fear was that they were being pulled back into her circle of influence, hard. But the more he knew about the situation unfolding in Manchester, the less convinced he was that Nat had even made her way back to Ben Turner. He fancied that she'd cut herself loose of the situation upon discovering her back-up had gone. She was a hard woman, but she wasn't hard enough that she'd take on Turner and his team alone. No, whether he had his own team with him or not, Turner wasn't acting with Nat here. She was hard, but she wasn't heartless. Only a real rucksack would take a cripple hostage.

The unfortunate part of all of this, and knowing what he now knew, was that too much time had gone without telling Grady and the others what they knew about Turner, about their own dealings with him. It had started as an uncomfortable secret, but became easier to keep as time passed. The same sort of feeling when you hadn't called a friend or relative for a while, and life went on, as much as you had a guilty feeling about the lack of communication, it was simply easier not to do anything at all. He, Jacques, Barnaby and Kenneth had all had much the same opinion on the matter, keep quiet, just get on with it. They'd agreed that Nat couldn't be involved in this, and that cutting her loose could go on being a regrettable, but no less necessary action if they wanted to live anything like a normal life. Of course, when they got there then there'd be the small matter of recognition when Turner laid eyes on them, but then it would just have to be Gerard's job to make sure the man didn't get time to make even the slightest peep. There was just the small matter of Grady's personal vendetta, and the insatiable need for revenge.

"We've got a signal again, it's weak but it's there," Euan said from up front beside his son, and Grady who was driving, as the van rolled into Tintwistle, a small hilly village just outside Manchester. It was the kind of place that emptied at the time of the regime change. Everybody moved closer to the epicentre of Network connectivity. Nobody wanted to be in a poor connection area when every aspect of existence relied so heavily upon the strength of it. Euan continued to scroll through several screens, searching for news, tutting in frustration at the speed of the data transfers.

"Any news?" Grady asked, impatiently. Euan let out a contemplative and non-committal hum.

"I don't think so, no. I can't see that any crews have got there yet, there's definitely nobody claiming to be, but that's not to say there's nobody there."

Ryan Bracha

"We better get a spurt on then, eh?" Grady grinned, "oh man, I can't wait to get my hands around Turner's jackin' neck, it's time for him to pay the jackin' piper!" Gerard felt his eyes roll involuntarily. *This time, it's personal.*

The threat of mutiny.

"Sir. There are ten minutes until Ben Turner makes whatever wild claims he has about you, and as yet there are no crews within touching distance of the building. The closest at present are a team of eight, calling themselves, the, *Network Ripping Crew*, approximately twenty minutes until they can take him off air."

"That's not good enough, Green. Why did we not enlist any Manchester based crews?"

"I'm afraid that we had no volunteers from that area. The north west, if you'll forgive me for saying, sir, is the region which seems to have taken to protestation against your rule more than the others. Turner seems to have done his homework."

"You're walking a fine line, Green. Be careful how you tread your next steps."

"Sir, I'm merely stating that Turner has chosen an area which works in his favour, because of the regional tendency towards mutiny against your rule. When Carter and his, ehm, gang, made their move, it was Manchester and Liverpool which were quickest to follow him."

"_"

"With respect, sir, I think we're focussing on the wrong aspect of this. Ben Turner is going to make his broadcast, whether we like it or not, and he's going to do it to a massive audience. Whatever it is that he has to say, you should move quickly to distance yourself from such scurrilous claims."

"Why should I? My people will dismiss his revolting words as soon as they leave his filthy lips."

"I'm not so confident that this will be true, sir."

"Are you doubting me? Are you seriously doubting my influence? Do I actually have to remind you what I've done for this country?"

"No, s-"

"I will NOT have my reputation, *my lifeblood,* talked down, *to my face*, by you, a useless serf."

"As you wish, sir. I shall return when you've calmed down, and realised that this is a very serious threat. The future of this country, *your country*, hangs by a thread, and you seem intent on handing Turner the scissors by transferring your frustration on to me. I respect your authority, and everything you've done for the people of New Britain. I will love and serve your country until I draw my last breath, but please, take my advice, and see that this is a very real threat to everything that we know. I am going to make contact with the crews, to see what plans they have for this situation. I shall return."

"Green!"

"-"

"GREEN!"

When I do bad things.

I'd followed Ben around the flat in that two hours. Watched as he rapidly pulled canisters of fuel from the holdall. Tennis balls with fuses protruding from them. Very crude looking devices. In the middle of the room the worsening figure of Johnny Stiff twitched erratically in his wheelchair. He'd not said anything for a while, simply focussed on his own plight. There was nothing he could do to help himself, whether physically, or with words. He seemed to have hit a serene plateau, and remained there. Like he'd accepted his fate. I almost envied the kid. My own life continued to become an endless myriad of unanswered questions mixed into a pot of brutality. Ben refused to tell me what they did to my father. Asked me again to trust him. Told me that everything would become clear before long. Once we had done here then he wouldn't ask me to follow him. Phase three was really only halfway through his big plan, but he only needed my help to this point. I wouldn't let it drop though.

"Ben, I need to know," I said, "tell me what they did to him."

My father died in a car accident, a year or so before the bomb that changed everybody's lives. He was alone, coming back from a conference in London where he'd been to discuss the positive effects of immigration on our country, and he'd been hit head on by a drunken lorry driver who'd taken the wrong exit to the motorway. He died instantly. It was big news for a while. The red tops had come down hard on the Eastern European driver, and by extension, the recent influx of Bulgarians with their country's acceptance into the EU. It had been paraded as ironic that he had been killed by the very people whose rights he was fighting to protect, and increase. Instead of the positive aspects of it that he so richly deserved in death, my father's name became synonymous with the negative side of things. Political parties with aspirations of taking Britain from the EU jumped on the bandwagon, racism and intolerance were then added to the roster of cynical terms that became attached to my father's name. I suppose at that time I should have come out and defended his name, but I didn't. I threw myself into my work, and I did everything I could do take my mind off of it, buried the news, and concentrated on retaining happy memories of the good man that my father was, despite what the left wing would have you believe he was, and what the right wing wished he was.

"We don't have time Nat, seriously," Ben said as he passed two bottles to me, "empty one all over the kitchen, and put the other over there," he said, pointing to the window ledge. I finally snapped. I felt myself drifting out of my body. Like I wasn't in charge anymore. Like when I. When I do bad things.

Katie Carter.

The signs for Manchester had begun to appear beside the M6 motorway a while back, and with the obscene speed they rattled south at, they weren't far at all from their destination to the north of the city.

"What time is it?" Garner asked of anybody.

"About four," said Katie, looking to the American cartoon character watch upon her wrist. Another sneaky little rebellion against her country of birth. "Won't Davie's men be setting off soon?"

"Not yet, two or three hours maybe," Carter said, conscious that they'd spent just a little too much time messing about in Edinburgh. Katie had kept on at him to visit Maguire before they left for Manchester, in a better-to-be-safe-than-sorry capacity. Carter had insistently declined the request, again reiterating that theirs was not a violent mission, and that they had no need for the weaponry, nor had they the time at all to waste. For her peace of mind, Carter had added a knife to their scant belongings fetched on the trip, but hoped that it wouldn't be needed.

"You know when we get married Paul Carter?" Katie said absent-mindedly, to a wide eyed response from her boyfriend.

"Married?" he asked.

"Yeah, married, you know how women take the names of their husbands?" she said, ignoring the question.

"I suppose, yes," he laughed.

"Do you mind if I don't get called Katie Carter? It sounds funny. It would be like being called Rebecca Bracker. Bric a Brac. Katie Carter. Kitty cat. You know? It's a bit too..." she said, drifting off, searching for the right word.

"Alliterative?" Carter offered.

"I don't know what that means," she said, "but I'm sure you're right. I want to stay called Katie Fleming."

"If, and when, we get married, you can have whatever name you want, Kitty Cat."

"Cool, I knew there was a reason I loved you Paul Carter," said Katie, dropping a hand onto his knee, before she turned her head to address Harry, "you're quiet in the back Mr Garner."

"Deep in thought, my dear."

"Well don't go too deep or you'll never get out," she said. Garner emitted a doubtful hum.

"I fear that it may already be too late for that."

Now is the time.

"People of England and Wales, those cheeky spies south of the wall to Scotland. And you, people of America, getting this shit fed back to you from those sneaky weasels bunked up in their little hidey holes. Don't act surprised that I know you're there, how was Lodge ever likely to be able to contain the whole country? There's satellites up there, for fuck's sake,"

Ben said, pointing to the ceiling above him, "there's zero security on the coast, so it's not beyond the realms of my imagination that it's a free for all in and out of Liverpool, and Newquay. Let's face it, it's all one big piss poor operation, run by a mass-murdering bastard with an ego the size of my massive balls." Ben reached down to grab a hold of said balls and give them a squeeze. Lips pursed into a self-satisfied sneer.

"He gives you some so-called *power* of judging your fellow countrymen, and you go mad for it. I took that power away from you and you went mental. Oh shit, did I say too much? Maybe, I dunno. Was it really me that killed all those law men? Made them shit their pants at the Scottish bogeyman and go on strike? Maybe, I can't take all of the credit though, I had a little help," he said, offering a mysterious smiling wink to behind the camera, "but my point is, what else has he given you? He makes you worship him, up in his ivory tower. He declares that everything he says should be gospel, and if you're not with him then you're against him. How the fuck is that a way to live? What kind of person thinks like that? A fuckin' despot dictator cunt is what. You know who else did that kind of shit? Bobby Lodge's own personal heroine, Maggie Thatcher. For you younger viewers, look her up. You know there's people *still* feeling the effects of the shit she pulled? The country starts to get back to something like cool again, then we let Bobby fuckin' Lodge onto the horse, and he does this to us." Ben paused, looked with some level of trepidation to behind the camera, and gave a thin smile. Sighed. Looked back to the camera.

"So let me tell you about some of the shit Bobby Lodge has done, taken directly from the diary of his one-time sidekick, Mr Harry Garner. It's supposed to be only read after his death. You know? So he don't have to pay for his crimes? Well, he's not dead yet, he's alive and living the high life. Don't ask me how I got it, because I won't tell you. But here, take a look." Ben moved forward to the camera, holding up the written and signed disclaimer from the author. Advising that it was indeed the posthumous journal of Harry Garner, in which he would catalogue the atrocities committed by Robert Lodge in his time on Earth. Ben pulled the diary back around and opened it up.

"Okay? Nineteen eighty six. Robert asked me if I'd like to come on a short trip with him and some of the others. He said that they made it every few weeks, to various towns and cities. On these trips they made it their work to murder foreigners, usually West Indians or South Asians. They said it was a way of cleansing our country one- Ooh, can I say this word? Should I? Shit man, okay, they said it was a way of cleansing the country one nigger at a time. They said that the threat to our British way was strong, and that the black bastards ought to learn that Britain is a dangerous place to come to. That they really ought to stay where they are. I politely declined the first trip, but peer pressure is really quite awfully strong. I joined them on their next venture, to Nottingham, and I have to say it was a lot of fun. Murdering parasites, who suckled, uninvited, on the quickly drying teat of Great Britain, was a lot of fun. By nineteen ninety, we had cleansed the country of close to two hundred of them."

Ben's eyebrows raised, an amused glint in his eyes as he addressed the nation.

"That's just the first page."

Five minutes away.

Only the sound of the engine was audible beneath
Ben Turner's speech, as each one of them hung on his
every word. Grady's eyes bulged in fury as he allowed
Turner's hatred and disrespect for Robert Lodge to
work its way into his psyche like an infection. So
what if their leader had done that? Surely he was well
within his rights to delete the foreign rucksacks from
existence. It was they who were in the wrong, leaving
their native land to come and try to leech a few
thousand quid from Grady's native land. They
deserved everything they got.

In the back, Gerard's heart pounded heavy
with a sneaking suspicion that the face behind the
camera that Ben occasionally acknowledged was Nat.
The look in his eyes, it was the look reserved for
somebody for which you held affection. It certainly
wasn't any of his group of Scottish reprobates. He'd
silently confirmed with Kenneth that he too had this
same suspicion, and felt his hand instinctively dart to
his jaw, rubbing the growth of hair. This was likely to
end very badly.

Euan eyeballed his son nervously throughout
the video. The kid was a sucker for a rousing video,
and was particularly free-thinking. He'd always had
friends of every culture before the bomb, and when
the regime change came about, he'd been devastated
when many of them left the country. That said, he
idolised his dad, and if Euan had thought it right to
stick around and defend the country of their birth,
then he would be happy with that decision. Just now,
though, upon hearing the first revelation by Ben
Turner, he could see his son wincing upon hearing
the N word, and subsequently, the news of what their
leader had done. Nicky had looked to him with a sigh

of disappointment, and all Euan could muster was a reassuring smile, and a rub of the leg.

Revelation number two.

"Nineteen ninety. The Gulf War. Robert and I had not been too happy to go into that one. It wasn't our war. It was helping the stinking Yanks get a stranglehold on oil. They repaid us by killing nine of ours in so-called friendly fire. We returned from the Middle East with an increased hatred of everything that wasn't British. Americans and Australians included. It didn't matter if you spoke the language. You weren't British so you had no place on our beautiful island. We began to attend protests and rallies on the quiet, and then in ninety six, we both left the army. He'd become fixated on joining the British National Party, and he wanted me as his right hand man."

Ben paused briefly, looked to the camera.

"You already know all of this part don't you? Let's skip forward a bit. Blah blah blah, dirty foreigners, blah blah blah, our beautiful country, and here we are. Robert looked straight at me as he wrapped his hands around the popular MP's neck. He'd said that this was the first step to getting our feet on the political ladder. Kill Terry Grayson. Eliminate the competition before you even throw your hat into the ring. There was a rather large funeral for the man, and then within weeks there was an election. Robert opted not to stand for the BNP, instead going in as an independent. I was the man behind the man. I paid off, threatened, or killed anybody that stood in his way. He was voted in by a landslide."

Two minutes away.

"So he was a little corrupt, who gives a jack?" Grady sneered, "can you tell me a politician before Robert Lodge who wasn't?"
Nobody said a word.
"See? You can't!"
"Oh, I thought the question was rhetorical," Jacques piped up, to the apparent mirth of his friends.
"Shut yer jackin' mouth, idiot!" Grady snarled. Being patronised was the worst feeling in the world. "You silver spoon suckin' maggot!"
"Oh fuck off Grady, you buffoon," Jacques yawned, to the absolute shock of the four men up front. They were crew members, and The Guidelines dictated that not even they would be permitted the use of profanity. Grady, shocked into silence, simply pulled the van to the side of the road, and quietly climbed down from the van, and approached the door by which Jacques sat. The low rumble of the sliding door followed, before Grady made a grab for the posh boy, pulling him from his seat, and laying into him. The other posh boys all leapt to his defence, tugging at the arms of the flailing crew member. Euan, Dopper, and Nicky in turn scrambled from their seats to make plays for Jacques' friends. The eight man ruckus spilled onto the road. Grady reeled as a well-placed butt from Jacques' forehead threw stars into his eyes. Dopper, a behemoth of a man, held Kenneth tight into a bear hug which threatened to burst every blood vessel in his body simultaneously, like the tiny individual balls of a blackberry, crushed within a balled fist. Seriously, that tight. Gerard pounded a fist to the nose of Euan. Nicky swung an athletic boot hard into the beanbags of Barnaby, dropping the snobbish rucksack like a sack of potatoes. In the

midst of the tussle, they barely noticed the faces of three ghosts drift past them as their car swerved to avoid hitting any of the pre-occupied scabs.

It can't be.

Carter twisted his head to try to get a better look at the rumble behind them. His face melting into apprehension.

"What's up, Paul Carter?" Katie asked, noting a concern in his eyes.

"I thought I saw somebody," he said, turning to his girlfriend, "but it can't be."

"*What* can't it be?" Garner queried from the back.

"I thought I saw Becker's silly sidekick, Grady, but I thought he'd gone soft and gone underground."

"Wilson Becker?"

"I don't know any other Beckers."

"Why would he be here?" Katie snorted.

"I don't know. Unless he just happens to live here, and partakes in a bit of bare-knuckle fighting, he might just have joined a scab crew. He and Ben have history."

"What's Ben got himself involved in Paul Carter?" Katie asked, more than just a little concern in her words. Carter sighed, and unbuckled his seatbelt as the car arrived at its destination, a few hundred metres from the property. There were no people around at all. But in the windows around them, a hundred or more were illuminated with that trademark blue, flicking and flashing. As Carter placed a hand on the door, Garner tapped his shoulder.

"Don't you think it'd be better if we stake it out a minute first? We don't want to rush into this. Believe me," said Garner. Carter paused. Pulled back his hand, taking the advice of the more experienced man. Katie slid a hand across to hold onto his. Carter stared out across the road toward the house. It didn't feel right. Ben was in there, and if that really was Grady back there, then it was only a matter of time before their paths crossed, which made things a hell of a lot more complicated for Paul and the rest of them. He accepted that rushing in might be a little amateur, but the longer they waited the more likely it would be that Grady et al showed up. He'd give it maybe two more minutes before going in.

"I'm firing my phone up, Paul Carter," said Katie, "I wanna see what Ben's saying."

Garner fidgeted nervously. There was going to become a point when he had to deal with this pair. He needed them to get to Ben, but at some point he would have end them. That was the deal. He just hoped that they'd go ignorant of anything that incriminated him.

"-sure time's against me, so let's skip forward a little bit," said the face of Ben sparkling out from Katie's mobile, using a stolen profile, since her own had been deleted forever, "I agreed wholeheartedly that the Prime Minister had to go, he was far too soft on immigration laws. We'd watched the Polish, Romanian and Pakistani cancer eat the country from the inside. He simply allowed it to continue. He had to go." Ben smiled at the camera. "Although I disagreed with how it should be executed, we couldn't trust anybody foreign. Robert continued regardless. He went to the Arabs."

Katie looked up to Carter, wide of both eye and mouth.

"What's he talking about?"

Garner felt the world drop beneath him. Although Turner hadn't named him directly yet, it would

Ryan Bracha

become very apparent. His stomach rolled. He needed to be calm.

"It sounds like he's-" Carter said, but cut himself off as the image of the door to Johnny Stiff's flat opened. From their vantage point, they could see a woman, carrying a person over her shoulder. It was a little too far away to guess what age. Across the head of the person it looked to be a surgical mask, or builder's mask. The woman hauled the person to a car that was parked just closer to them, threw the body into the back seat, talking to whoever it was. Then she closed the door, and returned to the building. As the door closes, voices emerged from behind the car. The fighting gang.

"Stay as still as you can," Garner muttered, eyes darting left and right to try to get a better view of the potential enemy.

Each one of the car's occupants remained frozen still, none of them wanting to attract unwanted attention.

Get clucked.

"No!" Grady shouted as he stormed forward, away from the following crowd. "No!"

"But surely we need 'em?" Dopper reasoned.

"It doesn't matter anyway Dopper, we're only coming along to watch Grady fuck it up," Gerard laughed, a bruised fist, battling for pain supremacy with the broken tooth.

"Get clucked!" Grady whined. It wasn't supposed to be like this. They were supposed to take Ben Turner down. He should have had the respect of his team. The stuck up bandstands, swearing like animals. His gut said they were cool, though. Maybe he really had bottled it? No. Not Grady, he'd show them all. He'd show them now. It didn't matter how many of them there were. He didn't need them. He had the power of absolute and pure hatred for Ben Turner.

"Face it Grady, you're a born loser, no amount of posturing could make you anything but," Jacques goaded.

"My back is fine, rucksack!" Grady roared, turning to face his mockers, "Straight as an iron rod."

Jacques also stopped, questioning Grady with a confused smile, as to the seriousness of his response, before deciding it was stated as serious. Jacques creased up in laughter, enjoying this new found confidence around Grady. He really was just a clown, all mouth and not a stitch of trousers.

"I meant-" he started, but he was knocked for six by a heavy club of a thump from Dopper, who already had Euan and Nicky surrounding him to ward off any potential vengeance.

"Just lay off him okay, you don't wanna do this then stand back and watch, I'm with Grady, you southern cornflakes, and you say another word to him I'll knock youse out, okay?"

Grady's beanbags grew instantly, coming back to the others.

"Thanks, Dopper. You heard him, you sit back and watch the professionals do it. You two coming?" Grady said, nodding to Euan and Nicky, who shrugged at one another. It was likely to be a hell of a lot more difficult with half a crew. But. Robert Lodge *had* promised anything they wanted.

"We're in," said Nicky, sharing a smile of solidarity with his dad. Grady grinned now at the four posh rucksacks.

"So now you're gonna see how the professionals do it, come on lads. Let's do it."

Ryan Bracha

"I play the events of the next few minutes out quickly in my head, breaking it down to bullet points for brevity's sake."

- "They told us the Royal Family had gone in the bomb. It couldn't have been worse news. That wasn't part of the deal. We loved that family with every being of our existence. It stood for what being British was all about. It was supposed to be the Prime Minister, and a few hundred people. But they took it wider scale, and they killed our Royal Family. The Prime Minister hadn't even bothered to attend, claiming illness. It was all for nothing. Robert was furious."
  Ben closed the book. Looked up to the camera solemnly, and shrugged pitifully.
- Katie stared, perturbed, at Paul Carter. Her eyes flicking just slightly behind them toward Garner, whose fists by now were clenching in expectation.
- Grady strode purposefully across the road, followed eagerly by his three remaining men. The loyal ones. They'd be rewarded for that when this was all over. There was nobody around. All the bandstands way too comfortable to leave their houses, just watch it all from the comfort of their armchair.
- "So, there you go. The big secret. Your leader, one Bobby Lodge, he murdered your old leader, and he murdered your Royal Family, and his good friend Harry Garner helped him every step of the way. He probably killed a few of your friends too. It was a very popular occasion. Was your mum there? Your boyfriend? Your kids? How does that make

you feel? I know you'll be sold a bunch of shit about it being all a big fiction. But you mark my words. The right people are gonna see this, and they're gonna get you out. Back to the freedom you forgot you wanted. Oh, and by the way, if you wanna get yourself a little freedom a touch earlier, I'd head to Scotland. You have no idea how much bullshit you've been fed about that place. Believe me, it's untouched. If you want real freedom? Head to Scotland. Tell Davie Craig that Ben says hi."

- An inner battle, there were two very big situations going down, and Carter needed it to slow down. They were in the car with a murderous racist, but at the same time there was the small matter of why they were here in the first place. Ben, and the four men who were stalking across the concrete to attempt an ambush on the report. Katie's phone had gone quiet.
"What's happening?" Paul asked. Katie looked up blankly.
"Nothing, he's not there."
Paul tugged it gently from her grasps to take a look. There really was nothing. Ben hadn't signed off at all. That wasn't like Ben. The situation had escalated further. Carter cursed himself for allowing it all to go along as it had. Now Garner sat in the back of the car that he shared with Katie. Part of the reason their lives had exploded as they had. The reason Katie's parents were killed, the reason Carter had to kill to be free of it. Katie's hand shook just a little as it grasped her knee. In front of them the men thumped hard against the door.

The speakers of Katie's phone rattled out an echoed version of events.

- "Network Ripping Crew! Get down!" Grady roared as Dopper slammed a boot into the door, ripping it from its aged hinges. He skipped around Dopper and into the room, rushing forward to the computer. Sitting atop the desk with a modern computer and web cam set up. Not the kind of place he'd expect at all. A very poor set up considering the popularity of the guy. Behind him Euan, Nicky and Dopper tumbled into the room.

"Where is he?" asked Dopper, eliciting a disdainful sneer from Grady.

"Let me just check my x-ray vision, I'll see if I can see through the walls," he spat, "I don't know where he is, look around, idiot!"

A sudden voice ripped them from their bickering.

"Boys! Easy now!"

They each spun in turn to see a figure, dressed in a too-big leather coat, and upwards of that a gas mask. Beside him stood a smaller, slimmer, more feminine figure, no less concealed by her own mask.

"Who, the jack are you? Turner? Is it you? Take your mask off you pansy!" Grady squeaked in rage. As he stepped toward the pair, he was jolted down to Earth before his foot even hit the ground. He twisted and squirmed briefly, and then lay, stunned. The smaller figure threw the Taser down toward Grady. Euan was positive he could hear her laughter.

"Grady? Well, that's an unexpected bonus, awesome. Sorry boys," said the muffled voice of the taller figure as he turned to the others, pulling a bottle from his bag, bringing it high to his face as he brought a gas lighter to meet it, his accomplice did the same, before he spoke to them again, "wrong place, wrong time, I guess. Next time put your money on a horse that's less incompetent than this piece of shit."

- From the door there came that familiar grey puff and swirl of smoke bombs. Obviously Maguire-crafted. It bugged Carter a little that Ben didn't think he could come to him with this. But then, he reasoned that he'd probably only try to talk him out of it, no matter what dirt he had on Garner, it could have been dealt with better. Through proper channels, like Davie Craig. The windows of the flat glowed a bright orange suddenly. Fire. Carter opened the car door, before stopping suddenly to watch what happened next, as two people strode calmly from the billowing smoke and approached the car which the girl had dumped the body into. Ben was the first to rip off his mask, beaming a massive smile toward the smaller figure. Probably the Nat Sweeney character he'd volunteered to come and take out. The girl's mask came off too. She screamed high into the air, a guttural release from deep within. Her mask was cast down to the floor, and she climbed into the car alongside Turner.

- Grady's skin bubbled, crisped and flaked as his corpse lay crooked on the floor of Johnny Stiff's burning flat. A combination of paralysis from the Taser, smoke inhalation, and the

direct hit that Ben Turner's petrol bomb had
scored dictated that he didn't stand a chance.

Three flaming figures.

Gerard couldn't believe his eyes. Nat had gone in with
Turner all the way. The pair of them working
together to try to take down Lodge. She'd gone so far
as to kill Johnny Stiff in the process of trying to
achieve whatever the hell she was trying to achieve
by getting involved. It was nuts. He could see, even
from this distance that she hadn't changed. That
carnal side to her which seemed to be getting ever
more present in her. She dropped herself into a car,
and the engine grumbled into life.
"Quick," said Gerard, get down."
The four of them scarpered. Gerard and Kenneth
followed one another into the tall grass which filled
the abandoned park. They ran just deep enough to
avoid being seen, and also just deep enough to
discover, and then trip over, a series of obstacles
made entirely of murdered people. Jacques and
Barnaby disappeared into an alleyway opposite the
park, one which seemed to only disappear to stairs.
There was no thoroughfare for them to escape from if
this went bad. From their spot they watched the car
carrying Ben Turner and Nat Sweeney roll by, and
from behind them, three flaming figures appeared,
flailing their burning limbs around. One of them
grabbed the other, throwing him to the ground.
Where it started as a potential fire-wrestling
situation, it became quickly apparent that it was
Euan, rolling his son along the floor, dousing the
flames, and then agonisingly doing the same for
himself. The bigger one, evidently Dopper, continued
in a panicked aimless run, eventually dropping to his

knees in agony. His squawks of pain doing their level best to ensure they'd stay with Jacques forever. Suddenly, a car revved into life to his right. He looked directly at the driver, and immediately knew who it was. Jacques stared at the driver speechlessly, as the car reversed along the road, flipping harshly to the right, and then heading off in the direction that Ben and Nat had gone. To his left, Dopper melted painfully away onto the pavement. Euan and Nicky were involved in their own drama. Jacques couldn't see that Grady or the cripple had got out. A shame. He was a funny kid. The cripple, not Grady. Grady was a dick. He walked out onto the road, bidding Barnaby to do the same, before they entered the grass that their friends had disappeared into.

"Gerard, they've gone," he called into the urban rainforest, "where are you?"

"Here," came a voice, which he followed, eventually hitting a small clearing, in which he found several things. Two, were Gerard and Kenneth. Another four, were the fresh and terrifyingly bloody corpses of some teenagers.

"Do you think *she* did it?" Jacques asked, as he approached the bloody mess.

"Let's face it, she's done worse."

"So what do we do now?"

"Lodge said we could have anything we want if we took them down. That was our ticket out. But after Turner spilled all of that I don't know that we can trust a word he says. I hate to say it, but we might just have to go and take what they have, and make it our own leverage?"

Jacques wanted to give an opinion but an awful flashback clambered onto his back, stepped up on his shoulders and then smashed a ball hammer directly into his face.

Ryan Bracha

"Oh no," he said, the realisation of the gravitas of the recent revelation.

"What?" asked Gerard.

"Carter. Paul Carter."

"What about him?"

"He's here. He saw everything. He followed Nat and Ben."

"Carter? What the hell is he doing here?" Gerard barked. Had Carter been watching them all of the time? What did he know? Gerard had had enough of being some piss poor player in this game. Always in Nat's ridiculously violent shadow. Never in the know. That dubious honour had always dropped squarely in Monty's lap. Even in the bedroom she was the dominant one. He didn't understand truly why he kept going back to it, but he did. One major factor was that the pleasure always outweighed the considerable pain. Even now, when Grady had taken this circus on the road, parading their crew as the future of law enforcement. It was never going to work. For one, Gerard had not stepped out of Nat's shadow to drop into that of another paymaster. That's why he didn't enter that flat. Not because Jacques had brilliantly goaded Grady and burned their bridges on their behalf. He was never going to into that flat. He was here to prove that he had the beanbags. He had the *balls*, to do this. He wasn't here to follow any more. He was here to lead.

"Fuck it," he said, "we know where they're headed, Carter can follow them, we can follow Carter. We have the jump on all of them. We don't leave until we have that book in our possession."

ONE MONTH AGO

It had been four weeks since the last war had ended.
Another few thousand lives pointlessly wiped out.
Edinburgh continued to wander about its business
like nothing had ever happened. The New British
armies had been defeated, but Lodge simply spun it
into his own favour. He told his people that they'd
been successful in their mission to stem the flow of
the savages from Scotland, despite the fact that the
Scots didn't even *want* to visit the diseased nation.
They had no option but to believe him. The country
was again working together toward a better future.
They seemed to appreciate that they needed to
knuckle down and accept it if they were to get to that
one unified objective of protecting their land. The
name of Paul Carter had been all but erased from the
minds of the drones. This was perfect for Garner.

   Lodge would now be able to rest in his seat of
complacency. His country now depleted further still
of potential dissenters. All that remained seemed to
be compliant hosts to take his tainted words and
make them fit into their own ideas. Those people, and
the law, who followed Lodge without question. The
crew members held the most coveted positions in
society. They were held in esteem by normal, law
abiding citizens. It was they who brought criminals in
to provide the solid entertainment of judging. Then
something happened. It hadn't happened since Carter
disappeared from the public eye, and triggered the
second British War. A crew was attacked. Two of
their men were killed. It was apparently very brutal,
or so said Garner's well-paid contact cum PI. A
woman, with the help of six men, had attacked them.

Spouted profane Scottish insults and goaded their paymaster. Then again, and again. The most recent of which was last week. Another crew. Another two men. Another woman with the help of six men. Garner kept it to himself. Pushed the contact to make further queries. Who was the woman? What was her angle? He hadn't heard from Davie that there was a mission going ahead, nor from the others. This looked to be a completely independent operation, with independent motives. They stayed in the shadows, worked with much more stealth than Carter's improvised mess ever did. They did the job and they got out, leaving just a clue as to what they wanted. The crews would never reveal that they'd lost men. Robert Lodge would never come out and tell the country that they had anything to worry about. A worried country became a volatile country. A volatile country became a very big worry for Lodge. The woman and her people were allowed to simply appear and disappear at will, picking off the law.

The contact had returned to him with names, to which Garner could himself put faces to, albeit with faces which would have aged five years since he'd last seen them. He couldn't believe it. Not least the beanbags they were displaying by their flagrant acts. The word came back from the contact when she killed again. She spoke with a very convincing Scottish accent, and killed without mercy or any hint of a second thought. He couldn't believe it. She'd always been so meek. So dainty. She'd always been more interested in money, in entertaining her flash friends. A total opposite to her staunch father. What the hell was her angle? Garner was intrigued, and more than just a little pleased to be able to cauterise some old wounds.

Garner put together a file of his findings -or more specifically those of his PI contact- and a written proposal for exactly how to stop the decidedly un-Scottish rogue element stalking through the streets of New Britain killing in the name of Scotland. As the last of the papers were clipped into the document, Garner left the house, stopping only to knock on the door of Davie Craig.

CHAPTER TEN

Not the least bit cute.

Ben screams a victorious roar into the small confines of the car. It makes my ear drum rattle just a little bit. It serves to knock my senses just a little back on track. We did it though. We got out of there. We did what Ben set out to do. I want to know what's in that book.

"You fuckin' beauty!" Ben yells, "we made it germs boy, you pleased?"

Johnny, from his spot, his horizontal spot on the back seat, croaks a response but I can't make it out.

"I say we dump this goon at a hospital and get back to base," Ben says after a short time.

"What's in the book, Ben?" I ask, I'm not fucking around now.

"You heard what were in the book, you were there," he says, obviously trying to dodge, but knowing full well that I won't leave it.

"You said you'd tell me, now tell me."

He bites his lip a little bit. It's not in the least bit cute.

"Lodge and Garner," he says. "Look, you've got your ticket out of here now, you know where the ferry is," he says, quickly trying to change the subject.

"Lodge and Garner what?" I say. *Come on you arsehole, just spit it out.*

"Just fuckin' read it, yeah? You want to know so much, just fuckin' read it." He pulls the book from the bag that he's laid across Johnny's prone body. "It's somewhere around-"

"Two thousand and eight, I know."

I flick the pages back and forth, through scores of sheets of written word. This is a whole library of confessions and massive evidence against Lodge. I find the beginning of that year and skim, looking for my dad's name, and then it's there.

April 2008.

Robert and I had encountered Bart Sweeney before. On a rally in Bradford against the South Asian disease which had been sucking at its veins for decades. Across the way we saw Bartholomew Sweeney holding up his banners, declaring that we were racist, swinging a video camera around the crowds. Jeering us. We were still aspiring to a getting any kind of a step onto the political ladder at that point, so when Bart Sweeney shoved his camera into our faces. I'm afraid to say we lost it a little. Robert forcefully removed the machine from his hands, and thrust it to the ground. Bartholomew swung for Robert. I pushed him away and punched him hard in the face. We were split up by the police and pushed back into our corners. But I'll never forget that look in his eyes as the officers dragged him away. He was just another lunatic left-wing piss-ant spoiling for a fight with anybody they could goad into responding. Animal testing, homelessness, rights of the dirty immigrants, left-wing lunatics will fight for anything. Everything is their cause. I think they only did it to hide from the fact that they were piss poor at the important things in life. Things like stability.

Bartholomew was different, though. He came from money. He was educated in Paris, and Oxford. He climbed the ranks at the opposite side to us, turning the whole thing from casual interest right up into lucrative career. Although he didn't opt for a livelihood in politics, his reputation in law was second to none. We were suddenly threatened by a malevolent presence. He was a threat to our ideology. His works and his seminars incited people to accept what was happening at the borders. He rallied the socialist elements to make a stand against our ethos. He pushed his face right into the world, and started slathering about peace to anybody that would listen. With his awful goody-two-shoes act he would show up on political television programmes, spouting his message of idiocy. He was unbearable.

We'd planned it for a while, following his diary retrospectively, to see how he operated, looked ahead to future appearances for an opportunity. It came unexpectedly, when he'd suddenly appeared on the television. Some local fluff interviewing him about what he was doing in such a small town. He was there for a few days for a conference. Robert called up to demand that I use this as my opportunity to shine. To take the piss-ant out of the game all together. What could I do? I stepped up. I paid a fee of £20,000 and a litre of high end Vodka to an immigrant named Piotr to drive his lorry directly into Bartholomew Sweeney's car. He'd agreed based on my promises of a lenient sentence, but of course I'd pulled some strings to ensure that quite the opposite occurred. There's a certain irony in my contempt for his actions. We had him killed in prison some months later. He was a horrific man.

With Bartholomew Sweeney gone, we'd moved on, but continued to keep a hand in with public perception of the man. A few distorted images of him in attendance of shady meetings, a handful of e-mails manipulated to show a darker side. Tabloid editors will swallow as much bullsherbet as you feed them as long as it's seasoned tantalisingly with scandal. I don't even feel remotely guilty about Bart Sweeney, or about what happened to him. He was a very poisonous man, and he stood for everything that Robert and I did not.

Moral superiority.

It's all here. Everything they did to my father. I'd felt a swirl of pride for him wash over in that prickling way that it does, from the face and neck all the way down to the fingertips. He was a good man. This tells me everything I already knew in that sense. He fought for people in general. He fought for the little person, even though he didn't need to.

A tear threatens to burst loose of its prison behind my eyes. My lip quivering just enough for Ben to notice.

"You cool?" he asks, not taking his eyes from the road. I nod. I can't speak. I need to digest this.

Robert Lodge, and his sidekick lackey Harry Garner. They destroyed my father, his name, his legacy, his reputation. My life. For power. They destroyed all of that for control of a tiny, formerly significant country with a population rapidly dwindling from its own perceived moral superiority over each other and the rest of the world. I flick back to the pages and re-read them. And again. My hatred for Lodge bubbles up quickly and violently, replacing the pride and hurt I'd previously been harbouring. "Where did you get this?" I ask. Ben looks to me. "Harry Garner, who else?"

"How? Where did-"

"He came to us. In Edinburgh."

"Edinburgh? Why Edinburgh?"

"You heard what I said back there. It's untouched. There's no Network, there's nothin' except people gettin' on with it. Why would we *not* want to set up shop there? Lodge fed us all a ton of shit about it bein' fulla cannibals and savages. He just wanted to keep us caged below the border under his piece of shit regime."

"Does it say how-" I start, already opening the book to search for clues but Ben cuts me off.

"Nah, Garner doesn't mention it. He didn't know. He was as surprised as the rest of us. That's what he said anyway."

The sound of Garner's name sticks in my ears like a knife, and an anguish punches me in the throat. I want to say something about it, but the car suddenly screeches to a halt outside a low orange building. A faint glow pulses through the windows. A browning faded sign declares it to be a medical centre near Hyde. I wasn't paying any attention to where we were going at all. Ben gets out of the car and opens the back door.

"Okay, germs boy, this is your stop," he grunts, pulling the whimpering funny man from his place on the back seat, "I'm sorry you had to get involved, but I needed your audience. I'm sure you'll be back on your wheels in no time, and then when it's all done with you'll be dining out on the humour of your near-miss with death for years. I basically did you a favour. Fuck, there'll even be a movie about you when the country goes back to how it was."

Johnny says nothing, just wheezes and whimpers his way through the ordeal of being dragged out, hoisted over Ben's shoulder, and then being dumped in the doorway of the medical centre. I toy briefly with the idea of taking my coat out and offering some kind of protection for him, but Ben is back in the front seat before the notion has even finished reeling through my mind, and is spinning us out of the car park and back on our way to Sheffield.

A safe distance.

They'd been following from a safe distance as Turner and his accomplice freely traversed the streets of Manchester, heading toward the M67 motorway. Carter began to get a very good idea of which direction they were headed in, until they'd come off at the Hyde junction, which threw his speculations into doubt. He'd feared that they'd got wise to the tail and were doubling back to avoid being caught, but hadn't picked up speed or attempted to drop into any of the estates with the narrow streets. They just continued on, before pulling in to a car park, which forced Carter to slow, and then stop, as they watched Ben pulling the same figure that the woman had dumped into the car back at Johnny Stiff's residence, out of the back, and dropping it carefully onto the ramp before what looked like a medical centre, leaning into the figure to give a soft slap of reassurance to the face. The whole event took less than a minute before the car squealed away.

"What do you reckon Paul Carter?" Katie asked, "do you think that's Johnny Stiff?"

The figure shivered in the distance, curled up and twitching on the concrete in the doorway to the medical centre. It was certainly feasible that it was the comedian. The thin, frail body, little movement. They had to do something. Carter shunted the car into gear and slowly approached the body.

"What about Turner and his little friend?" Garner asked as the car slowed. "Won't they get away?"

Carter sighed, pinched the bridge of his nose, and turned to the older man in the back. Garner hadn't said a word since Ben had done his big reveal. The issue had grown quite rapidly into the white elephant in the car. Carter and Katie had opted not to follow it up, both silently hoping that they could be reunited with Ben before it came back up.

"I'm not sure you get a say in what happens any more, Harry," he said, "I really don't know what your angle is here, but I'm pretty certain that I don't like it." Carter turned to his girlfriend, and nodded beyond her to the body on the ground, "go and take him to the front desk, tell them you found him here."

Katie nodded. Said nothing. Slipped from the car, and proceeded to lift Johnny Stiff from the ground with her hands hooked tight beneath his armpits. As she dragged him through the double doors Paul Carter addressed the man in the back through the rear view mirror.

"So, what's the angle?"

Ryan Bracha

Garner's face hardened. Of course he was in a bit of a bind here, but he'd never bottled a dispute in all of his life.

"I'm sure I don't know what you mean," he sniffed nonchalantly, "I'm here simply as moral support."

"Like hell you are," laughed Carter derisively, "what was the girl to you?"

"Girl?"

"Nat Sweeney. It was you that offered her as the target."

"No, it was simply that I identified her, she became a target all by herself."

"But you were so desperate to send a team after her. What was she to you?"

Garner exhaled, long and hard. Shook his head.

"It wasn't *her* that I wanted dead. She would have just been a bonus."

August 2009.

The day after we'd overthrown the Prime Minister. That very next morning. Robert called our team into Southwark for a debrief. There were myself, Robert, Rupert Green, Tony Devine, and Jacob Stanningley. Robert spoke of his next move as the new leader. He said that the people of Britain needed a true leader. Somebody who would direct them as required. He said that they were all empty vessels which needed to be filled with the right thoughts. He'd spoken of

our troops overseas. Said that they needed
to come home. Home. We agreed. Our
country could now become our own
again.

Through the next few weeks, the
plans became more solid. Robert
commissioned British businesses to
dismantle the airports, and seaports. Told
them they could take what they wanted
as raw materials. He'd used the tabloid
papers to issue ultimatums. Get out or
stay in, the choice is yours. This is all
really rather well documented though. It's
common knowledge. I fear I'm wasting
time and ink. The main issue lay with
the law. So many different human rights
lawyers coming at us telling us we were
break enough laws to put us away for a
long time. We couldn't have that. What
about the extremist towel heads across the
world be-heading their people and being
celebrated for doing so? What about the
crazed Texans frying their criminals, or
the entire United States free to wander the
streets fully armed with a gun that they
could purchase at the same time as their

alcohol? What about North Korea and the lunatic in charge? All of these factors were thrown back at the lawyers. Do something about that, and then maybe you'll have a leg to stand on here, we'd said. It got so that Robert despised lawyers and their ilk. One afternoon, we had become quite drunk, and got quite animated at the idea of lawyers being redundant. The country was still half in and out on his policies, and we needed that one thing which would bring them beneath our power in their droves. Then it happened. Social media. The country's unrequited love affair with talking to people through their computers. The news had become incessant regurgitations of something which had happened or was said on social media web sites. There were no such things as sound bites or interviews anymore. Celebrities, politicians, the police, they all communicated with the world using one hundred and forty characters. Popularity was how many followers you had, friends were thumbnail images, and influence was how many upturned thumbs your post could amass. It was perfect. It killed two birds with a single stone.

There was the matter of my brother, though. He was a part of the very institution that we were looking to dismantle. Although we'd drifted apart through the years, so much so that we no longer sent cards at Christmas. I couldn't help but feel a sibling's obligation. I offered him a role within our regime, and he politely declined. He disagreed with what we were doing. Unfortunately, Robert felt that if he wasn't going to go along with our plans, then an example would need to be made. He knew too much. Donald begrudgingly came along, but it was one hesitation too far. Robert endeavoured to destroy the organisation that he'd built up with Montgomery MacFarlane, a hard-nosed solicitor with an impeccable record. That MacFarlane had once been a professional cohort of Bartholomew Sweeney merely served to add the proverbial cherry to the top of the cake. The original plan had been to make them all redundant, force them to leave the country. Our nation had once displayed a proud approach to law and order, but that lawsuit philosophy made popular by the dirty Yanks had been seeping into the system like sewage into a pure and clean spring. Nobody was able to go about their business without the fear of offending or injuring somebody inadvertently, and then be subsequently sued for everything they'd worked hard to achieve. The money for nothing ethos that coated society like a thick layer of sleaze. Lawyers were to blame for all of that. People wouldn't even need to attend the courts. No win no fee. Stay at home. Money for nothing. It burned us up. So rather than cast the lawyers out, we kept them. We dangled the carrot of a fantastical future in New Britain, and when the doors were closed, we then stripped them of their every asset and we set them to work manual jobs, hard jobs. We showed them what real work looked like. Then with the reluctant help of my brother, we rolled out the change to the law. It was the major selling point to The Guidelines. Stay at home, stop it with the profane language, don't be violent, love your country, judge your fellow man by your own British standards, and the rest. You know what they are. In the war with Scotland my brother was forced to fight on the front line, and within weeks he was dead. Killed by the hand of David Craig. I can't say that I missed his incessant griping.

Trying to make sense of it all.

"Why did Garner come to you? Of all people?" I ask, closing the book around my thumb, which remains at my last point of reading. Ben snorts a small laugh.
"He didn't. He came for Carter. Thought he could help him take Lodge down. Wanted our help. Asked us to get him in with Davie Craig," Ben says, with an unexpected spit of jealousy when he says Carter's name.
"What made him think you'd be the people to help him?"
Ben shakes his head. Shrugs.
"I dunno. We were the big thing that'd fucked the country up a little bit I reckon. We were his best shot at getting back at Bobby Lodge for cuttin' him loose. He didn't tell us anything about that," he says, nodding toward the diary, "he just said he had information that could take him down. Then Lodge declares the second war on Scotland, Garner fights

alongside Davie Craig like they're best buds, an' it gets kinda swept under the rug. After that he comes along to all the dinners an' meetin's we have with Davie, like he's one of us. You'da asked me back then I woulda said he was just a weasel who dropped lucky. Then I found that. He wasn't lucky at all."

"What do you mean?"

"It doesn't matter. I'd found it, and I read it from front to back over an' over again. Workin' on what I can do to get it out there. Then one day, about a month ago, me and Paul get dragged along to a meetin', an' he's there puttin' bugs up Davie's arse about how there's this gang killin' law men in England," he pauses here to look pointedly at me, "an' he'd got word that it was a gang of old lawyers, doin' it all in the name of Scotland. Carter's name gets bandied about too, so Davie thinks it's summat to do with us. We plead ignorance. We've been livin' our lives up there, what would we want with law men? We got out an' we're staying out, right?"

The tops of the moors pass us by, and there's a light dusting of snow flickering in air. I listen to Ben as the flakes skitter and dance in front of the window.

"But then Garner drops this file onto the table. He's been doin' some homework. This particular gang of lawyers are known to him, he's dealt with 'em before. He pulls your old boy with the tash's name out of his arse, an' it's one I know from the book. Montgomery MacFarlane. Says that it's bad. You were all trouble. You could cause Davie Craig some issues. That's when I figured summat weren't quite right. Like, I figured he was playin' us for dickheads. Then the picture of you comes slidin' out, and well, you *know* what I did with that."

I feel a roll of my stomach just allowing that thought to knock at the door to my consciousness, so I hold my hand up.

"Don't start, you were doing so well too."

Ben grins, and rolls his eyes. Holds out two fingers in front of my face.

"Here you go, smell yourself."

"*How old are you?*"

"Old enough," he smirks, satisfied that despite the serious turn our acquaintanceship has taken, he can still hit the buttons. "Anyway, where was I? Oh yeah, the file. I saw my in. It were like a golden opportunity to make my stand. Paul had done his part, he'd set the country up. He'd pulled the last safe piece of the Jenga tower out, an' it would be up to me to make sure that tower tumbled. He's my best mate an' I love him to bits, but the truth of it is that he doesn't want change. Now he's got Katie all he sees is what's at the end of his nose. As long as they're okay, he won't worry about anybody else. He didn't fail me, but for all the potential he had, I reckon he failed himself. I'm the one who sees the bigger picture. I see the damage that Bobby Lodge is doin' to everybody. I saw what you were doin', an' I have to say I was impressed."

"Flattery will get you nowhere."

"But I was. I wish I'd thought of it first, but I didn't. You did. I saw somebody who might just want the same things as me. You bein' an absolute treat for the eyes was just a bonus."

"My previous statement still stands."

"Hah!" he barks. "So I volunteered for the job. I volunteered to take a team down south an' kill you. At least that were the official line. I had my own motives, and my own plan, all of which started with takin' *that* from Garner's room." Again he nods at the book.

Ryan Bracha

"How does it end?" I ask. He smiles, and his fingers grip tight onto the wheel as he pushes down onto the accelerator as a sign by the road tells us we're in Derbyshire.

"It ends with me takin' Bobby Lodge out of the game all together."

Coming clean. Sort of.

"All I told you was that I knew who they were. Do you think I asked them to act as they had? Please tell me how you think I might have managed to orchestrate it so that a team of lawyers who hate my guts would kill people at my behest?" Garner asked, incredulously.

He was growing tired of this already. If only he'd squeezed out of the pair where it was that they thought Turner was headed then they'd both be dead by now. He needed to buy time.

"Really, Carter. Regardless of what you've heard, I'm not a bad person. I'm on *your* side. I want to see the back of Robert as much as you. I just saw an opportunity to take out an old enemy, for old times' sake."

Carter eyed the older man doubtfully in the rear view. Katie skipped across the car park from the doors to the medical centre, drawing a more subdued demeanour to the retired revolutionary, wanting to keep this low key in the presence of his girlfriend.

"Four hundred people died in that bomb, Harry. Forgive me for doubting your credentials as a good person."

Garner said nothing. If Carter wasn't going to push the matter then neither was he. Katie seated herself beside, and smiled at, Carter.

"All done. They took him straight away. We need to get out of here though, they said they were calling the police."

Carter smiled at her affectionately. Squeezed her leg. Then eyeballed Garner once again with a stare that told him in no uncertain terms that this wasn't done with. *No, it's not over yet*, thought Garner as the car urgently rolled out of the forecourt, *not by a long chalk.*

Meanwhile, bringing up the rear.

The news that Johnny Stiff had been found alive at a medical centre in Hyde near Manchester, and that two bodies were found at his flat were crew members who'd crossed the picket line, was released not long before Gerard and the rest were to be found speeding along the M62 and wasting no time in switching to the M1 south en route to Sheffield. The van had a subdued air about it but it wasn't without its discussion.

"So let's go over this again, what do we know, and what can we glean from it? What are we missing?" Jacques asked, a droning tiredness in his voice, he was seated alongside Gerard in the driver's seat. Old habits dying hard. "Bullet points please."

- "Nat's with Ben, but they don't have the comedian, he's in hospital," Kenneth offered.
- "Two of that lot of funsters are dead, we don't know who, but we can probably guess that they're Dopper and Grady," said Barnaby.
- "Paul Carter is here, but we don't know why. More than likely in cahoots with Ben." again from Barnaby.
- "And Robert Lodge is a big gherkin, very probably responsible for the death of the

Ryan Bracha

Royal Family. We know this because Ben has Harry Garner's own personal journal." Gerard muttered across to him.

"Is that everything? What are we missing? If we go in there half-cocked we're going to screw it up," Jacques said, gently bashing his head against the window, before rolling the window down, and lowering his head out of it, eyes wide open and willing the cool air to wake him up a little. The battering of the frosty moorland wind bit into him in a not entirely unpleasant way, and whilst it wasn't exactly a series of intravenous shots of espresso, it did bring about him an alertness he'd been missing for days.

"How did Turner get hold of that journal?" Gerard asked. It was a good question. "What does Harry Garner have to do with all of this? Other than he's got a lot of blood on his hands?"

Jacques let out a low hum of contemplation. It was quite plausible that Garner was dead, and was being tarnished posthumously.

"Let's say he's dead. Let's say that Turner and Carter killed him in Scotland. They discover the diary. They then conspired with Davie Craig to send Turner down here with a gang of idiots to try to smear the blood all over Robert Lodge. To do that they come for us-"

There was the question. How did they know about theirs and Nat's efforts? Jacques paused. How did they know? There was no answer coming.

"Why us? What do we have to do with anything?"

"I was wondering the same thing," Gerard muttered, "if they're headed where we think they're heading I suppose we'll get our answers soon enough."

ONE MONTH AGO

"I wanna do it, I wanna take a crew and cut these fuckers down," Ben said, a resolute stony glaze coating his eyes. The four heads twisted toward him. The first one to speak was Carter.

"Really? Why?"

"Well, why not? Mr Craig here has been almost *too* kind with his hospitality. I'd like to be able to repay him in some way, and what do you get for the man who has everything?"

Four blank faces.

"Revenge," smiled Ben, "you get revenge."

Garner watched the trio leave the room. Ben Turner twitching an eager and excitable dance and shadow boxing with the girl who giggled along with the ridiculous show.

"I have to say that was an unexpected bonus," Garner said, looking to the Scottish leader, "I thought it might be more difficult to convince him than that."

"Aye, he's pure radged. Might be just as well sendin' a couple ay extra boys doon there with him, just in case, likes."

Ben scrabbled up the stairs, leaving the other two to wander through to the kitchen. It could only be a matter of time before Garner came scurrying home to see what they were up to. Keeping tabs on them. He bounded up to the attic room, before carefully stepping over Garner's regimentally tidy belongings, dropping to his knees and, mindful of the man's attention to detail, lifted the edge of his mattress and pulled the book from beneath it. Ben smoothed the edges of the sheet around the mattress, hoping that it would at least buy him a couple of days.

The team that Davie had put together assembled themselves on the lawn of his front garden in the cool January morning air. They were a collective of men who'd impressed him with their loyalty to the cause. Garner watched them considerately. They weren't exactly the kind of crew that he would put together personally, but Davie knew his men and he knew what they could do. The perennially intoxicated brother wandered aimlessly through them. "Atteeeeeeeeeeeeeeen. Hut!" he laughed, pulling a joint from his lips as he stood to attention, slapping his free hand down hard against his thigh.
"Roan, man, fuck off the now mate," Davie said admonishingly, "tryin' tae get these boys' heads in the gemme eh? Cannae well fuckin' dae that wi' you actin' the clown."
Roan chuckled away, pulling more weed into his lungs, and wandering off toward the back garden, singing music that Garner recognised from his youth, but couldn't put a name to. Something American.
"Boys," Davie said, clapping his hands to bring their heads back to the here and now, "there's a very real threat tae the Scottish way ay life, an' youse are gonnae put a stop tae it."

"Ben? Whit's up?" Maguire asked, his eyes flickering around behind Turner, looking for the usually ever present sight of Paul or Katie, neither of whom were around.
"I need a favour, mate," said Ben as Maguire ushered him into the long hallway of his home. Young Paddy bounded through to greet him.

"Ben!" he laughed, throwing his arms around Turner's neck, but searching around for his best friend, "where's Katie?"

"Now then Paddy, she's away with Paul, she says she'll come to see you soon," Ben said, releasing himself from the youngster's grasp and standing to address Maguire. "I don't suppose you've any supplies goin' spare?"

"Whit dae ye need 'em for?" Maguire asked, a suspicious tone to the question, given that Turner on his own was a most unusual encounter. Ben allowed a smile to creep across his face, just a small one, and he directed it to Paddy before turning to Maguire. "It might be better saved for somewhere a bit more private."

The team had grown restless. Turner should have been there an hour ago. The tall ginger one that had been earmarked for first aid duties played cards with the youngest member, using the bonnet of one of their cars as the deck. Two of them had sneaked off in the direction of Davie Craig's stoner of a brother. Garner watched them share a few drags on his cigarette, and the trio spoke animatedly to one another. *This*, was supposed to be the team that took MacFarlane out, along with the insufferable bore that was Ben Turner. Harry Garner began to wish he'd kept the information to himself. Maybe taken a few weeks out to deal with the matter on his own. Now it was too late. Davie had briefed the men on what they were to do, tabs they were to keep on Turner, and ultimately what they were to do once that job was done. He'd made them repeat it back to him several times. Given spot check pop quizzes to check their understanding. They gave the answers required of them, but whether they could actually pull it off was the one question to which an answer remained to be seen.

Ben pulled up alongside the front garden of Davie Craig. There was a rag tag band of bampots and neds that had flitted in and out of his life at various points since he'd been in Scotland. Davie Craig seemed to trust them. Liked to surround himself with the insane. He didn't seem to do calculated and intelligent at all, he seemed to far prefer brute strength and fearlessness. Like maybe he thought he could just fight his way out of any sticky situation. With that in mind, Ben pulled the bag self-consciously tighter onto his back. Drawing his secrets closer. There was no way they could know that he held them, but there was that guilt. Beneath the surface there was anticipation. For weeks he'd been looking for his opportunity, and here it was. A few hours from now he'd be back in New Britain, with the key to its freedom, a holdall full of explosives, and the name and face of one very beautiful kindred spirit.
"You boys ready then?" he called over to them from the kerb.
"Are you sure you want to do this?" Carter asked him quietly, "It's not our fight."
Ben slammed a hard, but affectionate hand onto his friend's shoulder, and chewed at his own lip.
"Dude, I've never been surer, and you'd be surprised at how much of our fight this is."
"What do you mean?"
"Just trust me, and for fuck's sake, be careful up here without me. Don't trust any cunt."

The third of the cars rolled away and rounded the corner en route to New Britain, leaving the rest of them waving away thin air. Garner allowed a satisfied sigh to leave his lungs. The plan was underway. Within the next few days another part of his former life and several potential banana skins on the road to total freedom would have disappeared, clearing the path to focus only on Robert.

"So I guess that's that then, eh?" Katie said to Paul, arms swinging to keep warm. Carter smiled.

"Yes, I think so. Harry, are you coming back with us or making your own way?"

Garner, eager to hear any thoughts the pair had now their friend was unwittingly walking to his own death, opted to head back with them, and they left Davie Craig to his day.

There was an odd sense of deflation around recent events. The excitable air had dissipated, like that feeling people got just after Christmas. Everything built up to one event, and then afterwards, there remained an awkward unease about the question of *what now*? Davie Craig returned to the house, and seated himself in the lounge, holding tightly onto the large single malt he'd poured for himself. He watched the tidal movement of golden brown liquid in the tumbler, lost in his thoughts. If Garner called this right then the self-contained boil of irritation sitting right on Scotland's arse below the border would be lanced before long. An urgent rattattatting at front the door jerked him from his thoughts. Who the fuck?

"Mr Craig," said the bald man before him as he opened the door. Davie knew him. The teacher with the bomb skills who'd introduced him to Paul Carter.

"Aye?"

"It's Maguire," he said.

"Aye?"

"Ehm, aye. I need tae talk wi ye. It's aboot Ben Turner."

Ryan Bracha

CHAPTER ELEVEN

Back at the ranch.

We're scampering across the broken tarmac. The light is dropping rapidly as the evening creeps upon us, and the already familiar silhouette of the police station looms large over us. Neither of us speaks as we enter the building. We only focus on getting to cover, so that we can regroup.

"So, Mr Turner. Do you want to tell me *what phase four* is?" I say, lowering myself to the jumble of rags that looks to have once doubled as a bed. Ben seats himself in his usual spot by the table. Stares at his hands. Chews the skin on the inside of his mouth. Looks at me.

"I can, but I've got a feeling it could change very soon," he says, somewhat mysteriously. I jerk upright, cross-legged.

"How so?"

"We've been followed," he says, "an' I've got a feelin' the angel that's been missin' from my left shoulder is about to make an entrance."

"What do you mean?"

"Carter. He followed us to when we dropped germs boy off. I didn't see him again after that but believe me, he'll know where we were heading. He's my boy and I love him but he doesn't know shit about tailin' somebody."

"*Paul* Carter?" I ask incredulously, immediately feeling stupid when Ben snorts with laughter. I hate feeling stupid.

"Yeah, *Paul* Carter. How many Carters do you think I knock about with?"

"If he knows where we'd go why did you bring us back here?"

"We need to be on familiar ground."

"Why? If Carter's your friend, why did you not just stop and send him home? What does he want?"

"My guess is the Scottish contingent made it back to their illustrious leader an' he's been sent to bring me back. Either that or Garner noticed his book was gone. Or both. And if Garner knew the book was gone, then the chances are that he's tagged along."

My stomach launches itself without warning up into my throat, eliciting a gasp. Garner.

"Do you think Garner's here with him?"

Ben frowns.

"I really hope not, 'cause if he is then there's a very real chance that Paul knows what he's done, like, the stuff in the book, an' if he knows, then Garner knows he knows. You know? If it's gonna kick off then I want home advantage."

I do know, but in all honesty I couldn't give a flying fungus about Carter. Garner's the man for me right now. My eyelids flicker. A shortness of breath takes me over. I want to do bad things.

"If they're headed this way what are we sitting here with our thumbs up our arses?"

It's been a while.

The lights of the car sliced a fat line through the dusk, throwing a glow over the building. A flash of green demanding that they *Keep Britian Brittish.* To the right was Ben's car. Leaning on the bonnet, was Ben. Carter spun the vehicle around, drawing to a stop several metres from his friend, who lurched upright from his own car, stretched his arms out wide, and grinned. Carter and Katie each exited the car, slowly followed by Harry Garner. Carter watched the older man carefully, even as Ben approached with an affectionate smile across his face.

"Paul, glad you could make it, it's been a while. You brought Katie too, what a delightful treat!" Ben pulled Katie in close to him as she returned his greeting.

"So," said Ben as he stepped away from the trio, "to what do I owe this unexpected pleasure?"

"I think you know mate," said Carter, still remaining quite focused on Garner. "I've come to get you home, before you do any more damage."

"Damage to who? Lodge? Why should I give a fuck about him? He's the exact same cunt I'm *tryin'* to damage."

"No mate, to yourself. The girl you're in with. She's dangerous," Carter said, taking a second to look around the car park, "where is she?"

"She's gone, you just missed her. She's headed to Cairnryan. Gettin' a ferry out of here, I don't have any use for her now," Ben said, looking to Garner for a reaction. None came.

"What the fuck are we doin' here talkin' about *her* anyway? Did you not see my fuckin' broadcast? What the fuck are you still doin' here with *him*? You know what he's done, right?"

Carter nodded.

"I do."

"And?"

"We hadn't really come to that bridge yet," Garner piped up, "but what's say we speed forward a little and get to that blasted bridge?"

Garner deftly spun on his heels, swinging a heavy set of knuckles into Carter's kidneys, dropping him to the ground, before pulling hard on Katie's arm, dragging her close to his body. His right hand explored her clothes.

Ben Turner is a Dead Man

"Hey! Get off my tits, dickhead!" Katie said, emitting a yelp which quickly became a strangled gurgle. Ben's body immediately tensed to the situation. On the ground, his friend gasped painfully, reeling from the sucker punch. Katie violently threw her legs into the air, desperately trying to escape Garner's ever-tightening grip. Still Garner's hand ran across Katie's body. Blindly looking for the knife he knew she'd brought. Ben eyeballed Garner. Neither man blinked.

This was not the plan.

Nat watched the dramatic greeting from Ben from the shadows that played with the light at the edge of the car park. The beams of the car were casting a demonic silhouette across the valley behind him. She watched the couple getting out of the front of the car. Paul Carter and the girlfriend who looked at least five years too young for him. Carter was shorter than she'd imagined. Not by much, but given his reputation she'd expected well over six feet. Then *him*. He climbed from the back of the car. It took everything she had not to stomp over there, and then stomp out a merry dance on his face, but she couldn't. That wasn't the plan. They talked briefly, then it happened. Garner made the quite predictable move of making a grab for the girl. The punch to Carter's kidneys looked like a big one. He was only small but Garner was in good shape.
"Hey! Get off my tits, dickhead!" squealed the girl. Ballsy. She wasn't going easily. Nat picked her moment. Carter had managed to drag himself upright, and stood toward Harry Garner. Hands held out in surrender.
"Garner, come on, let her go," Carter pleaded. Ben shrugged.

Ryan Bracha

"Fuck him, like the fanny he is. He's not doin' shit Katie, trust me."

"Shut up, Ben. You're not helping," Carter said, "Harry, please."

"Katie, just calm down love, he's doin' nowt. Are you Harry? Come on, 'fess up, you don't have the balls."

Boom. The trigger.

Nat stalked on the balls of her feet as she approached the stand off. The flicker of her movement caught Carter's eye. A look of confusion. Nat flexed herself. Touched her toes. Pulled each arm above her head one after the other. Carter said nothing. Just watched Nat. Watched her breathe out, like an athlete, awaiting the starter's gun. Swinging her arms. Watched her take the first step. Then the second. The third was her last step, before the right foot swung hard, and heavy. Swooping down past the floor, and back up again, stopping only when her toes connected with a ferocious velocity, with the racist, corrupted, murderous balls of one Harry Garner. Immediately his grip on Katie was released, as she skittled out of his arms and into those of her boyfriend. Garner dropped to the ground, his hands instinctively fondling his injured beanbags. The man gasped. Wheezed. Squealed in agony. Nat hadn't finished. She lurched forward, pulled at Garner's hair with both hands, dragged him by it to the car, and opened the door.

"Nat," Ben said, a concern in his voice, as he looked to the embracing lovers, "what are you doin'?"

Nat ignored the question. Dropped the horrible cretin's head into the car's doorway, his skull against the seat.

"Seriously, Nat, this weren't the plan, what are you doin'?"

Slam.

Ben Turner is a Dead Man

The door thumped as it hit the resistance of Garner's face.

Slam. Nat began to wail.

Again it bounced back. Garner's nose was flattened and bloody against his face. His teeth smashed from his jaw. She roared at the man who killed her father.

Slam.

"Nat! Come on!" Ben's voice said from somewhere in her world. Nowhere that she'd care to visit. Just somewhere.

Slam.

Garner's skull cracked. Popped. A gush of blood and matter ejected across the car park . She didn't stop.

Slam.

Slam.

Slam.

"Nat!"

Slam.

Garner's corpse rolled from the doorway. The disfigured and unrecognisable skull flopped limp against the wheel, attached to a lifeless lump of a body. She felt arms grabbing for her. The roar in her throat rattled until it hurt. Until it was the only thing in her headspace. She stumbled back against the arms which pulled at her. Still she roared as the arms lowered her to the ground. The roar became a wail became heavy sobs that echoed around the inside of her head, and a dainty figure dropped to the floor beside her, and placed its arms around her. The sobs subsided, and a gentle hushing began to take root in her consciousness.

"So what *was* the plan?" a voice asked.

"That was. I just figured it'd be a lot more dramatic if I protested a little bit."

Nat laughed. A snotty, half laugh through the tears, but the first step to her mind becoming her own again. She looked up from the ground. Ben and Carter stood over her, a frown of concern on Carter's face. A malevolent smile on Ben's. Beside her was the girl, arms wrapped around her still. She was very pretty. Huge eyes which blinked away tears of solidarity for her.

"You're a bad ass you Nat Sweeney," she smiled, "a proper bad ass."

Here comes the cavalry. Part one.

Gerard took the car off the M1 at junction 31, heading for Mosborough. They weren't too far away now. A few miles at most. The sporadic streetlights punctuated their journey as they neared their destination.

"We could just leave it," said Barnaby, voicing a suggestion which all four of them had been close to making at various junctures along the way, but where would that leave them? Nowhere. Stuck in this country for the rest of their days.

"We could, but then what have we got? Nothing. We've been through far too much to give up now. There are four of us, and two of them," said Jacques.

"What about Carter? What if he's there?" Barnaby queried. It was a good, and valid question. They-

Lights.

From behind them an overwhelming amount of light smashed them into blindness. A rumble of several vehicles. Overhead, a low flying helicopter sliced through the sky. The symbol on its side had to have been a fake. It *had* to have been. A trick of the blinding light. The van swerved to avoid being hit by the speeding convoy which descended upon it like a vampire. To the right, a much more modern vehicle than the old Transporter they were travelling in, blacked out windows and pristine black paintwork, pulled up alongside them. With the assault rifle trained on Gerard's head, he had no choice but to pull to the side of the road. With eight assault rifles trained on all four of them, they had no choice but to climb solemnly from the van, drop to their knees, and await their fate.

Here comes the cavalry. Part two.

The helicopter hovered over the car park, the four figures which stood in it, and the apparently headless figure which bled an ocean across the concrete.
Down below, Ben looked suspiciously to Carter.
"What the fuck's this?" he shouted, fighting a losing battle with the roar of the chopper, "what the fuck, Paul?"
Carter shrugged.
"I don't know," he bellowed, "I have no idea, honestly!"
Suddenly a screech of tyres against concrete howled into the night. Behind them a familiar sight. The idiots. The Scottish idiots. The same Scottish idiots that Ben had sent back to Davie, fucking, Craig. He was being fucked over.
"You're in with *them?*" he screamed, "with those fucking clowns?"
Carter shook his head.
"I have no idea what's going on, Ben!"
"Fuck you, *mate,*" Ben said, not angry at Carter, just disappointed. Katie began to shout things too, but the slowly lowering chopper drowned her out. Without taking his eyes from his friend, his former friend, Ben removed Garner's journal from his bag. Around them cars began to spill into the forecourt of the police station. He pulled several pages from the book, and

passed them to Nat with a smile. She'd got her man. He pulled several other pages from the diary, and stepped to Carter. Thrusting the pages into his hand, Ben pulled his friend close, kissed his cheek, and spoke into his ear.

"You fucked me over Paul. I can't believe you fucked me over for Davie Craig. Take a look at this shit an' think about reassessing your loyalties, prick."

Ben pulled away from Carter, smashed a heavy forehead into his nose, and bolted. From the dark of the bushes which spilled down the hill and into the distance, Ben turned to take one last look at Nat, caught like a deer in headlights as Carter reeled from the blow. The cavalry descended on her like piranha, each tugging at her arms to secure her. From a distance there were men with guns aimed at the melee. He felt bad for leaving her, but he had a job to do. The helicopter lowered further, and as Ben threw himself head first down the hill and away from the action, the last thing he spotted on the side of the helicopter was a circular logo, one which bore the words *US Air Force*.

June 2011.

The attack on Scotland was just a front. Robert had been in bed with David Craig long before then. Long before the bomb. Just as we were staunch nationalists, Craig was exactly the same with his own country. They wanted devolution. They wanted their own parliament, and the Prime Minister would hear nothing about it. He said they'd be nothing without us. They didn't have the brain power to function on their own. That's what he'd intimated in the House of Parliament. Of course, Robert passed these opinions on to David Craig, and it rattled his cage hard. Craig was paid handsomely to bury what he knew about our involvement in the bomb, in exchange for power in his own country. It would work for everybody. Robert led the charge against our Prime Minister. He would take control of the country quickly, and subsequently, he would make a show of offering the hand of solidarity to Scotland. Each man well aware that this would be refused. To further cement his place at the head of our fledgling state, Robert launched an attack. This short and pointless war worked for both sides, as David Craig appointed himself as the leader of the Scottish rebellion, and when Robert would eventually call off the charge, Craig would himself be lauded as a national hero, saving his people from the

English. Both men awarded the power and independence they so greatly coveted.

David Craig partly financed the construction of the wall to keep the two ideologies apart, and life would go on, on both sides of the structure, however each man saw fit to run their worlds. I don't personally know exactly what happens up there now, nor do I truly wish to discover, but I fear that I must do so if I am to secure my own safety, away from the despicable and egomaniacal leader of New Britain. I lost my worth to him. If he has no use for me, then this is tantamount to anti-British behaviour, punishable by death. I will now make a pilgrimage to Scotland, also known as No-Man's Land. There I will search out people who can help. People who owe me, those who made my life what it has become.

This is all I know about Robert Lodge. This is a written confession of what I have done. It is a written testimony of what Robert Lodge has done, and of what he's capable of. I don't ever expect to bask in any kind of glory in life, or indeed death, for I am as guilty as them all, and deserve whichever punishment that fate sees fit. My only hope is that my words would put concerned minds at rest, as an answer to the questions they so desperately ponder.

THIS MORNING

Davie Craig watched as Carter, his girlfriend, and Harry Garner disappeared from the street. He'd given them a six hour head start. That should be enough to get to Ben, get him locked down and shipped off before he could say anything stupid. It would ruin everything. For Davie, the worst case scenario would be for the shitebags south of the wall to appear in their droves, on the run from Lodge and his crumbling empire, built on the sands of dictatorship. He just didn't get it. No matter how many times they'd spoken about this in the past, Lodge never really understood what being a leader was. His desire and objective was to rule. Nothing more. He wanted subjects who would hang on his every word. He didn't understand that being a leader was far more than that. You had to earn the respect of your people, not demand it. You had to make them want to work for you, not enslave them. Even now, when they'd spoken on the telephone previously, Davie would throw derogatory jibes at his counterpart. He wondered if Rab Lodge ever wished he'd never made the bet in the first place.

Davie strode proudly into his house, crossed the parlour with the tartan covered snooker table, picked up his telephone, and dialled.
"Aye, aye, naw, he's really fucked it up, naw I mean seriously fucked it up. I think it might be time tae intervene."
He replaced the receiver. Smiled. Picked it up once again and dialled a new number. He waited patiently, one foot tapping against the tiles which made up the

Saltire beneath him, as he whistled Flower of Scotland. Eventually the call was answered. He smiled once again, and eventually spoke.

"Mr Lodge, game over, that's a fiver you owe me."

EPILOGUE

"Sir, please accept my apologies for the humble nature of your lodgings. It is merely a temporary accommodation until this blows over, which I'm extremely confident it will do very soon."

"Tosh! I've slept in far inferior places in my time, what do you think I am, Green? Some kind of snob?"

"No, sir, I was merely-"

"You were merely nothing, Green. I don't know what kind of an impression you have of me, but do indeed rest assured that it is wrong! I cannot help but feel disappointment every time I gaze upon your sorry soul, Green. Disappointment. When this blows over, and I am reinstated as head of this fine state, your life will be the first thing I take. You mark my words."

"As you wish, sir."

"Green? What are you doing? Get back here, you ignorant fool!"

"-"

"Green? What the- Who are you? What have you done with Rupert?"

"I've done nowt with your mate, he's waitin' outside, you could say he was turnin' a blind eye."

"What? Who the blazes are you?"

"Me? I'm your worst fuckin' nightmare, pal."

BANG.

BANG.

BANG.

Ben Turner is a Dead Man

Afterword and Jackin' Acknowledgments

Thanks, as ever, go to my wife, Rebecca. It's been a big year and you've been awesome at every beautiful step.

Thanks to my baby girl, Delilah, for showing me what being a grown up looks like. You're the actual most best beautiful girl I've ever seen. Plus your tiny trousers crack me up. How can there possibly be people that fit in those?

Mark Wilson. Author, friend, and all around good egg (balls), for your unwavering belief in my work.

Keith Nixon. Author, friend, and all round ginger denial expert. The longer you fight for the strawberry blond army, the longer there'll be a bearded ginger named Keith in my books.

Thanks to Allen Miles, Craig Furchtenicht, Gerard Brennan, Darren Sant, Paul Brazill, Martin Stanley, Gareth Spark, Les Edgerton, Richard Godwin, Robert Cowan, and all of the other writers I've worked with or will work with in the future. The scene is absolutely rock solid right now and you're what makes it what it is.

Thanks, finally, to you, for picking up my work and giving me a shot at entertaining you. Give this book a review on Amazon for me, whether you thought it was good or shit. If you want to come find me on Twitter or Facebook and tell me how shit you think I am, I'll tell you to fuck off.

Ben Turner is a Dead Man

The finale of the ridiculously entertaining Dead Man Trilogy is due to drop in Summer 2015. That should give you plenty of time to go and look through my back catalogue.

I'd personally start with Bogies, and other equally messed up tales of love, lust, drugs, and grandad porn. It's hilarious.

No, no, maybe go back to the start and pick up Strangers are Just Friends you Haven't Killed yet.

You know what? Just get them all. Get Mark Wilson and Keith Nixon and Allen Miles and Craig Furchtenicht and, and, and.

Just go and pick up a ton of indie books and see what real storytelling is.

Ryan Bracha

Ben Turner is a Dead Man

Printed in Great Britain
by Amazon